Eternal Whispers

(Lena and Elias)

ISBN: 978-93-341-3994-5

Written by Divyam Agarwal
Cover Design by: Divyam Agarwal

Published by: Self-Published

Printed in India

For information about special discounts for bulk purchases, please contact the author at contact@divyamagarwal.com

Why **"Eternal Whispers"**?

The title "Eternal Whispers" encapsulates the essence of the novel's exploration of love, communication, and the silent struggles that often linger beneath the surface of relationships. It signifies the quiet yet profound conversations that happen between individuals—both spoken and unspoken—reflecting the deep emotional connections that persist even in moments of silence. The whispers represent the tender moments of vulnerability and understanding that foster growth, revealing that love is a journey filled with intricate nuances that resonate long after the words are spoken.

Plot Overview:

"Eternal Whispers" tells the story of Lena and Elias, two individuals navigating the complexities of their relationship against the backdrop of personal growth and emotional healing. The novel opens with Lena reflecting on her feelings of uncertainty as she stands on a cliff, contemplating the past and the distance that has grown between her and Elias. Throughout the book, Lena grapples with her emotions, writing a heartfelt letter to Elias to express her fears and hopes for their future together.

As the narrative unfolds, readers witness Lena's journey of vulnerability as she confronts her feelings of longing and confusion. The couple's connection deepens through open conversations, laughter, and shared experiences, gradually transforming the silence that once defined their relationship into a space of trust and understanding. The climax of the story occurs when Lena and Elias embrace their commitment to face life's uncertainties together, solidifying their bond.

The ending emphasizes their readiness to embrace the future, highlighting the importance of love as both a guiding force and an adventure. The novel concludes with a sense of hope, leaving readers with a reminder of the enduring power of love and the beauty found in communication.

Key Themes:

- Love and Vulnerability: At its core, "Eternal Whispers" explores the theme of love as a multifaceted journey marked by vulnerability and openness. Lena and Elias learn that expressing their feelings and fears strengthens their connection and deepens their understanding of one another.

- Communication: The novel underscores the importance of communication in relationships. Lena's letter serves as a catalyst for honest discussions, highlighting that words can bridge gaps created by silence and misunderstanding.

- Personal Growth: Both Lena and Elias undergo significant personal growth throughout the story. Their individual journeys toward self-discovery and healing contribute to the development of their relationship, demonstrating that love thrives when both partners are committed to growing together.

- Nature as a Reflection of Emotions: The changing seasons, particularly the autumn backdrop, symbolize the emotional shifts experienced by Lena and Elias. The vibrant colors and the beauty of nature mirror their evolving connection and the hope that accompanies new beginnings.

Plot Structure:

The plot of "Eternal Whispers" follows a traditional narrative arc, divided into three key parts:

- Introduction: The story begins with Lena's introspection as she grapples with her emotions and the distance in her relationship with Elias. This section establishes the emotional landscape and sets the stage for their journey.

- Rising Action: As Lena decides to confront her feelings, she writes a letter to Elias, sparking a series of conversations that reveal their fears and aspirations. Their deepening connection unfolds against the backdrop of autumn, filled with shared moments and reflections on love.

- Climax and Resolution: The climax occurs beneath the oak tree, where Lena and Elias confront their future together, ultimately committing to face life's uncertainties side by side. The resolution emphasizes their readiness to embrace the adventure of love, leaving readers with a sense of hope and anticipation for what lies ahead.

Character Development:

- Lena: Lena's character arc centers around her journey from uncertainty to empowerment. Initially, she struggles with unexpressed emotions and fears about her relationship with Elias. Through writing and open conversations, she learns to embrace vulnerability, ultimately finding the courage to articulate her desires and hopes for their future.

- Elias: Elias's character evolves alongside Lena as he confronts his insecurities and learns to communicate his feelings. Initially portrayed as supportive yet distant, he becomes an active participant in the dialogue surrounding their relationship, demonstrating growth through his willingness to engage in honest discussions about their future.

Symbolism:

- The Ocean: The ocean serves as a powerful symbol of the vastness of emotions and the complexities of love. It reflects the depth of Lena's feelings as she navigates the turbulent waters of her relationship with Elias, representing both the beauty and challenges inherent in love.

- Autumn Leaves: The changing leaves symbolize transformation and renewal. As Lena and Elias's relationship evolves, the vibrant autumn colors mirror their emotional journey, highlighting the beauty of growth and the promise of new beginnings.

- The Oak Tree: The oak tree serves as a sanctuary for Lena and Elias, representing strength and stability. It is beneath this tree that they confront their fears and commit to facing the future together, symbolizing their enduring love and resilience.

Emotional Impact:

"Eternal Whispers" elicits a range of emotions, from the heaviness of unexpressed feelings to the warmth of love and connection.

Readers are drawn into Lena and Elias's journey, experiencing the highs and lows of their relationship as they navigate vulnerability and communication. The emotional depth of the story resonates with anyone who has faced uncertainty in love, inviting reflection on their own experiences and the transformative power of openness.

<u>Ending Notes:</u>

The conclusion of "Eternal Whispers" leaves readers with a profound sense of hope and possibility. Lena and Elias's commitment to facing the future together encapsulates the essence of love as an adventure—one that is ever-evolving and filled with unexpected twists. Their story serves as a reminder that true love, rooted in vulnerability and communication, can weather any storm and create a lasting bond that transcends time and distance. With its heartfelt exploration of love and the whispers that connect us, "Eternal Whispers" resonates long after the final page, inspiring readers to embrace their own journeys of connection and growth.

Table of Contents

The Gallery

Lena stood in front of her painting, a vivid picture of the ocean, with waves crashing against the shore under a setting sun. She took a step back, allowing herself a moment to breathe. The exhibit was finally here—her chance to share her art with the world. The gallery buzzed with excitement, voices mixing with laughter as the colorful canvases filled the white walls.

The smell of fresh paint and varnish filled the air, blending with the scent of wine and appetizers. Lena had poured her heart into this collection—each piece reflecting her experiences, her hopes, and her fears. But as the guests wandered through the gallery, admiring her work, a familiar knot tightened in her stomach.

"What if they don't understand?" she whispered, fidgeting with the hem of her red dress, which stood out against her pale skin.

"Lena! You have to meet these people!" Her friend, Sophie, full of energy, grabbed her hand and pulled her into the crowd. Lena hesitated but let herself be dragged along.

"This is an incredible turnout," Sophie said, her eyes sparkling with excitement. "Your art deserves this. You're amazing!"

Lena smiled, though her heart was racing. "Thanks, but I'm just nervous."

Sophie squeezed her hand. "You'll be fine. Just be yourself. People will love you, I promise."

As they approached a group of guests, Lena put on a smile, ready to engage. But out of the corner of her eye, she saw something—or someone. A tall man stood near her favorite painting, the one that had taken her weeks to finish. It was a canvas filled with swirls of blue and gold, capturing the emotional chaos she often felt.

"Who is he?" Lena whispered, her heart fluttering.

Sophie glanced at him and nudged her. "I don't know, but he looks like he's thinking deeply."

Lena felt drawn to him. His dark hair was slightly messy, and his fingers gently brushed the frame of the painting, as if he were searching for something in it. He wore a simple black t-shirt and jeans, yet there was something elegant and confident about him.

"Excuse me," Lena said, gathering her courage. "What do you think of this piece?"

The man turned, and their eyes met. His piercing blue gaze held hers for a moment. "It's... haunting," he said, his voice smooth and calm, like music. "It feels like it's searching for something, just out of reach."

Lena's breath caught. "That's exactly what I wanted to show," she said, surprised at how honest she was being. "It's about love and loss."

He smiled softly, making her heart race even more. "You've captured it beautifully. I'm Elias, by the way."

"Lena." She offered her hand, and when their fingers touched, a spark seemed to pass between them.

"Nice to meet you, Lena." He held her gaze for a moment longer, and the unspoken connection between them felt powerful.

The noise of the gallery came back into focus, and Lena pulled her hand away. "What brought you to my exhibit?"

"I was passing by and saw the sign. I'm a musician, and art has always fascinated me."

Lena's heart quickened. A musician appreciating her art felt special. "That's great. Music and art... they connect in so many ways."

Elias nodded, and they continued talking. Their conversation flowed easily, touching on their passions, dreams, and struggles as artists. With every word, Lena felt a deeper connection growing between them, like an invisible thread pulling them closer.

But as the night went on, Lena felt the weight of her secret—her illness. It hovered over her, casting shadows on her thoughts. She wanted to tell Elias everything, to be open, but fear held her back. What if he couldn't handle the truth?

"I should probably go talk to the other guests," she finally said, needing a break from the intensity of their connection.

"Of course," Elias replied, his eyes showing he understood. "I'll be around if you need someone to talk to."

As Lena walked away, she glanced back at him. In his eyes, she saw something—curiosity, maybe even longing.

The evening passed in a blur. Lena smiled through the conversations, but her mind kept drifting back to Elias. When the night began to wind down, Lena stood by the entrance, thanking people as they left. When Elias approached, a small smile played on his lips.

"I enjoyed our conversation, Lena. Your art is really moving."

"Thank you," she said, warmth spreading through her. "It means a lot to hear that."

"If you're free, I'd love to see more of your work sometime. Maybe over coffee?"

Her heart skipped a beat. "I'd like that."

They exchanged numbers, and as he walked away, Lena felt a flicker of hope. Maybe, just maybe, she could let herself explore this connection, even if it was only for a short time.

As the gallery emptied and the lights dimmed, Lena stood alone, her heart still racing. She looked out at the empty street, the moonlight reflecting off the ocean waves, and whispered, "What if this is the beginning of something beautiful?"

The Musician

Elias sat on the edge of his bed, staring at his worn guitar leaning against the wall. The strings gleamed under the soft glow of the lamp, but no music came to him. His mind was filled with images from the art gallery—bright colors, people talking, and most vividly, Lena's warm smile. He ran his hand through his tousled hair, trying to shake off the memory, but it clung to him like the salty sea air outside his window.

"Get it together," he muttered. "You've got a gig tonight." He stood up and began pacing around his small apartment, cluttered with sheet music, empty coffee cups, and memories he couldn't escape.

As he got ready for the night, a familiar sadness washed over him. Memories of Lila, the love he had lost so suddenly, crept into his mind. They had shared everything—music, dreams, and a future he could no longer picture without her.

"Music is all I've got now," he sighed, picking up his guitar and strumming a few soft chords. The sad, soothing notes filled the room, wrapping around him like a comforting blanket.

Music had always been Elias's way to express emotions he couldn't put into words. With every note, he poured out his feelings, but since Lila's passing, the music felt heavier, weighed down by grief. Tonight's gig was at a small bar—a place that used to feel warm and welcoming but now felt lonely.

As he drove through the winding streets of the coastal town, the sun set, painting the sky in shades of orange and purple. It was beautiful, just like the painting that had captivated him at the gallery. Lena's face flashed in his mind—her eyes shining with passion as she spoke about her art.

"Maybe I should write a song about her," he thought. The idea both excited and scared him. It felt too soon to feel this way about someone new.

When he arrived at the bar, he unloaded his equipment, the weight of the guitar a familiar comfort in his hands. The crowd buzzed with excitement as regulars filled the room, their laughter blending with quiet conversations. The small stage, strung with fairy lights, was where Elias had spilled his heart many times before.

"Elias!" A voice called out, pulling him from his thoughts. It was Sam, the bar owner, greeting him with a smile. "Ready to play?"

"Always," Elias replied, forcing a smile. His eyes scanned the room, half hoping to see Lena. He didn't know why, but the thought of her being there made him feel lighter.

Taking the stage, Elias strummed the first chords of a familiar song, the sound filling the bar. The crowd hushed, drawn in by the music. He closed his eyes and let the melody take over, losing himself in the notes.

But as the song ended, his mind drifted back to Lena. What was it about her? She was different—vibrant, full of life. Her art had stirred something deep in him, and for the first time in a long while, he felt a flicker of something like hope.

Elias played through a set of his original songs, each one reflecting his heartache. As he sang, the weight of his past pressed on him, yet the thought of Lena kept surfacing. The girl in the red dress, with her contagious laughter, lingered in his mind.

After his set, he stepped off the stage, his forehead damp with sweat. He was greeted by familiar faces, but he felt distant from them, his thoughts still lingering on the art gallery.

"Great set tonight, man!" Sam said, patting him on the back. "You've still got that magic."

"Thanks," Elias replied absently, glancing around once more. He couldn't help but hope Lena might show up.

As the bar started to empty out, Elias finally let himself relax. He sipped a beer and chatted with the few patrons who remained. Just as he was about to pack up, the door swung open, and there she was—Lena. The dimly lit bar seemed to brighten with her presence.

Elias's heart skipped a beat. She looked around and spotted him, her face lighting up with a smile. A spark of energy shot through him as she walked over.

"I didn't think I'd find you here," Lena said, her voice like music to his ears.

"I just finished playing," Elias replied, trying to sound calm, though his heart was racing. "I'm glad you came."

"I wanted to hear you play. Your music at the gallery was beautiful," she said, sitting beside him, her eyes sparkling with excitement.

"I'm glad you liked it," Elias said, feeling warmth spread through him at her words. "I'm still trying to write something as powerful as your paintings."

They talked, their conversation flowing effortlessly. Lena told him about her journey as an artist, the struggles she faced, and the joy she found in her work. Elias shared his own experiences—how music had been both a friend and an escape.

The more they talked, the closer they felt. The connection between them was undeniable, magnetic. For the first time in what felt like forever, Elias felt a glimmer of happiness, a light piercing through the darkness that had surrounded him since losing Lila.

As the night went on, Elias wanted to know more about Lena—her dreams, her fears, her life. But he held back, unsure of how deep their bond really went.

"Can I show you something?" Lena asked suddenly, her eyes bright with excitement.

"Sure," Elias replied, curious.

She pulled out her phone and showed him a photo of a large canvas. "This is my latest piece. I'm not sure if I want to show it yet, but I'd love your opinion."

Elias leaned in, his heart racing again as he took in the bold colors and raw emotion in the painting. "It's stunning," he said softly, mesmerized. "You've really captured something here."

"It's about love and loss," Lena said quietly. "It's still a work in progress, but it feels like a part of me."

He watched her face as she talked about her art, feeling a surge of admiration for her talent and vulnerability.

Later, as they stood outside in the cool night air, Elias walked Lena to her car. "I'm really glad we met," he said sincerely.

"Me too, Elias. It feels like we've known each other forever," Lena replied, her smile warming his heart.

As they said goodnight, Elias felt a sense of possibility blooming inside him. "Maybe we could create something together—art and music," he suggested with a hopeful grin.

"I'd love that," Lena said, her eyes shining with excitement.

They exchanged one last look, knowing that this connection between them was rare and special. As Elias watched her drive away, he couldn't shake the feeling that this was the beginning of something beautiful.

The Unsaid

The sun filtered through Lena's bedroom curtains, casting a warm glow across the room. She lay in bed, wrapped in her blankets, thinking about the night at the bar. The laughter, the music, and especially Elias—he had entered her life so suddenly, reigniting a spark she thought had long gone out.

"What am I doing?" she whispered, running her hand through her tousled hair. The thrill of their connection excited her, but the weight of her illness hung over her like a dark cloud, threatening her new happiness.

After a moment, she sat up and reached for her sketchbook on the bedside table. It was her refuge, a place where she could express her emotions without fear of being judged. She flipped through the pages, filled with vibrant sketches and color swatches, her heart heavy with the thought of what she needed to face. "How can I let him in?" she wondered, gripped by the fear of opening up.

Taking a deep breath, Lena began to draw, capturing the feelings from the previous night—the way Elias had looked at her, the gentle way he spoke, the spark between them that felt both exciting and terrifying.

Outside, the world bustled with life, but Lena remained lost in her thoughts, consumed by the uncertainty ahead. "What if he finds out about my condition? Will he stay?" The questions swirled in her mind, leaving her uneasy.

Meanwhile, Elias sat on his balcony with his guitar, trying to write a new song. The soft ocean breeze played with his hair as he strummed the strings, his thoughts drifting to Lena. The way she talked about her art, the light in her eyes—it was like a wave of fresh energy washing over him, slowly easing the grief that had held him for so long.

"She's amazing," he thought, letting his guitar rest in his lap. But with every thought of Lena came the shadow of his past—memories of Lila's laughter, her warmth, and how they had shared everything—music, love, their dreams.

"Am I ready for this?" Elias wondered, caught between hope and fear. "Can I let myself feel this way again?"

As the sun began to set, casting shades of orange and gold over the world, Elias picked up his guitar again. This time, the music that flowed from him was soft and haunting, a melody filled with longing, love, and the fear of letting go.

Lena, still caught up in her thoughts, put aside her sketchbook and decided to take a walk. Maybe the fresh air would help her clear her mind. As she strolled through the small streets, the colors of fall surrounded her—golden leaves on the ground and the crisp scent of pumpkin spice from a nearby café. The beauty of the world outside only made the storm inside her feel heavier.

"You can't hide forever," she told herself. "If this is going to work, you have to be honest."

With every step, she rehearsed the words she needed to say. "Elias, I need to tell you something important…" The thought of rejection made her stomach churn. "What if he doesn't understand? What if he walks away?"

After what felt like an eternity, she found herself standing by the ocean. The waves crashed against the shore as she took a deep breath, letting the salty air fill her lungs.

In the distance, she noticed a figure silhouetted against the setting sun, and her heart leaped. It was Elias, sitting on the sand, his guitar in hand, completely absorbed in playing. His soft strumming mixed with the sound of the waves.

Lena hesitated, her heart racing. Should she join him? Could she be brave enough to tell him the truth?

As if sensing her, Elias looked up, his expression shifting from concentration to warmth when he saw her. "Lena!" he called out, smiling widely.

"Hey," she replied, feeling both relief and anxiety as she approached him. "I didn't know you'd be here."

"Just looking for some inspiration," he said, gesturing for her to sit beside him. The warmth of his presence made her both comfortable and nervous.

"It's beautiful," she said, looking at the horizon where the sun painted the water in gold. "Your music is beautiful too."

Elias laughed softly. "Thanks. It helps me deal with everything that's been going on."

"Me too," Lena said quietly, her heart pounding as she felt the need to tell him the truth. "I've been doing a lot of thinking since we met."

"About us?" he asked gently, his eyes full of understanding.

She hesitated, fear tightening her chest. "Yes, but it's complicated."

"Complicated can be good," Elias said, his voice kind and patient. "I'm here to listen."

Lena took a deep breath, trying to gather her courage. "Elias, I—" But the words stuck in her throat. The sound of the waves filled the silence, her thoughts overwhelmed by fear.

"I'm not good at this," she finally admitted, feeling vulnerable under his steady gaze. "I haven't been in a relationship since…"

"Since what?" Elias asked softly, leaning closer, offering her a space to speak without pressure.

"Since my diagnosis," Lena said, the words spilling out before she could stop them. "I have a chronic illness. It's something I've kept hidden, even from myself sometimes."

The air between them felt heavy and fragile. Elias's expression changed from curiosity to concern. Lena held her breath, waiting for him to respond.

"I'm so sorry," Elias said quietly. "How does it affect you?"

"It affects everything," Lena replied, her voice shaky. "Some days are good, others… not so much. I'm scared of the uncertainty, of what could come."

Elias nodded, his eyes never leaving hers. "You don't have to face this alone," he said gently. "I'm here. I want to understand."

Tears welled up in Lena's eyes as the weight of his words sank in. "But what if I pull you into my darkness?"

"Everyone has their own battles," Elias said sincerely. "I lost someone I loved deeply. I understand pain and loss. I just want to be there for you, Lena."

In that moment, hope flickered inside Lena. The walls she had built around her heart began to crack, letting in the warmth she had been keeping out.

"Thank you," she whispered, her voice thick with emotion. "I've been so scared to let anyone in."

"You don't have to be scared," Elias reassured her, his hand brushing hers gently.

As they sat together, the waves lapping at their feet, Lena felt a wave of relief wash over her. The fears and burdens she had carried alone now felt a little lighter. Maybe, just maybe, this was the start of something good, even with the shadows that still lingered.

"Let's create something together," she suggested with a small smile. "Your music, my art—we can blend our worlds."

Elias's eyes lit up. "I'd love that. It sounds like a beautiful collaboration."

They sat side by side, the sun sinking below the horizon, sharing their dreams, their fears, and a connection that seemed to grow stronger with every passing moment.

A Brush with Fate

The next few days passed in a haze of creativity as Lena and Elias grew closer through their collaboration. Each morning brought new ideas, and each evening, they met at the beach where the ocean's rhythm became the soundtrack to their work.

Lena stood in her studio, surrounded by splashes of color and the scent of paint. The blank canvas before her called out, but her mind was full of inspiration. She had never collaborated with anyone before; it felt both exciting and a little scary.

"What if I can't do this?" she wondered, biting her lip as she picked up a brush. But the memory of Elias encouraging her helped her push through.

"Just let it flow," she whispered to herself, remembering how he had played his guitar in the sunset.

As she began to paint, vivid images filled her thoughts—the warmth of the sun, the sound of laughter, and the spark of creativity that had ignited between them. She imagined a world where music and art blended perfectly, where their souls danced together through colors and notes.

After a few hours, Lena stepped back to look at her work. Bold streaks of orange and deep blue intertwined, representing the emotions swirling inside her. The painting was becoming a reflection of their journey together—filled with passion, light, and the shadows of their fears.

Her phone buzzed with a message from Elias: "Can I come by later to see what you've created?"

Her heart raced at the thought of sharing her art with him. "Of course! I can't wait to show you!" she replied, smiling.

That evening, as the sun began to set, Lena prepared her studio for Elias's visit. She tidied up her paints and brushes, wanting everything to be just right. Sharing this intimate part of herself felt both thrilling and nerve-wracking.

When the doorbell rang, Lena's heart skipped a beat. She opened the door, and there stood Elias, his hair tousled by the wind, a guitar slung over his shoulder.

"Hey! I'm excited to see what you've been working on!" he said, his eyes full of energy.

"Come in!" Lena led him into her studio, where the canvas stood partially covered in vibrant colors.

Elias stepped closer, taking it all in. "Wow, this is incredible!" he exclaimed, his voice full of admiration. "It really shows so much emotion."

Lena blushed with pride. "Thank you! I wanted it to reflect what we've been creating together."

"It's beautiful," Elias said, still staring at the canvas. "What's your vision for it?"

Lena took a deep breath, her heart pounding. "I see it as a journey. I want to show both the struggles we face and the hope that comes from creating together."

Elias nodded. "I love that. It's like the music I've been working on."

Lena's excitement grew. "You've been writing songs too?"

"Yeah, our conversations have really inspired me. I've got a few melodies that would go perfectly with your painting," he said, taking out his guitar.

He started to strum a gentle tune, the notes filling the room. Lena closed her eyes, letting the music wash over her, imagining how it would blend with her artwork.

"It's beautiful, Elias," she said softly. "Can we try something? You play while I paint, and we'll see how they fit together."

"Absolutely! Let's do it," he said, eager to start.

Lena picked up her brush, and as Elias played, she let the music guide her strokes. Each note brought her deeper into the creative process, allowing her emotions to flow onto the canvas in perfect harmony with his melody.

Hours passed in a blur of art and music. They were completely absorbed in their work, unaware of the time. Lena felt a sense of freedom, as if her emotions were flowing onto the canvas, dancing in time with Elias's music.

Suddenly, Elias stopped playing and smiled. "I have an idea," he said, a playful glint in his eye. "Let's mix things up. I'll play something unexpected, and you just paint whatever comes to you."

Lena felt a mix of excitement and nervousness. "Okay! Let's do it."

Elias closed his eyes and started playing a fast, lively tune. Lena couldn't help but feel energized by the rhythm. She grabbed her brush and moved with the music, letting go of any plan and painting freely. The strokes were wild and bold, reflecting the energy of the moment.

Their laughter filled the studio as they lost themselves in the joy of creating together.

When Elias finally stopped, both of them were breathless and grinning. "That was amazing! I've never played like that before," he said, clearly exhilarated.

Lena stepped back to look at the painting, her heart still racing. The colors were vibrant and alive, a true reflection of the music. "I can't believe we just did that. It feels so alive!"

"It does," Elias agreed, admiring the painting. "You captured the music perfectly."

Lena felt a deep sense of gratitude. "Thank you for pushing me out of my comfort zone. I really needed that."

Elias turned to her, his expression serious. "You're an incredible artist, Lena. The world needs to see your talent."

Their eyes met, and Lena felt a pull toward him, an unspoken connection that grew stronger by the moment.

"Elias," she whispered, "I feel like we're creating something more than just art."

He took a step closer, their bodies almost touching. "I feel it too. There's something special happening here."

The air between them seemed charged with emotion. Lena's heart raced as she realized just how much she cared for him.

"But…" she hesitated, her old fears resurfacing. "What happens when the music stops? When the painting is done?"

Elias gently took her hand. "Then we'll create something new. Together. That's the beauty of it."

Lena felt warmth spread through her as his words sank in. "Together," she repeated, a smile breaking through her doubts.

As they stood in the fading light of the studio, hand in hand, Lena felt hope blooming inside her. The fear she had carried began to fade, replaced by the excitement of what lay ahead.

"Let's keep creating," she said, her eyes bright with determination. "Let's make this journey unforgettable."

Elias nodded, his gaze full of promise. "I'm with you. Let's see where this takes us."

With their hearts aligned and their creativity ablaze, they knew they were at the start of something extraordinary—an adventure filled with art, music, and the deepening bond between them.

The Past Resurfaces

The following weeks felt like a dream for Lena and Elias. Their collaboration grew stronger, and soon Lena's studio was filled with art that matched Elias's music—each painting reflecting the melodies he played, each song responding to the colors Lena created. Together, they made something magical, a mix of art and music that felt like it needed to be shared with the world.

But despite the joy of creating, a quiet tension began to build—small at first, like a distant storm, but growing stronger each day.

It started with little things: missed texts, rescheduled meet-ups, and moments when Elias seemed distant, lost in thought even when they were together.

Lena noticed the change but couldn't figure out why. "Is something wrong?" she wondered, staring at the half-finished painting in front of her one afternoon. The bright colors that had once flowed so easily now felt stuck, trapped by her growing unease.

Meanwhile, across town, Elias sat in a recording studio surrounded by instruments and sheet music, but he couldn't focus. His mind kept drifting to Lena—her laughter, her vulnerability, the way her eyes lit up when she painted. She had become his muse, but with that came a pressure he hadn't expected.

His manager, Kara, noticed the shift in him. "You've been distracted, Elias," she said, looking through a folder of upcoming gigs. "We need to stay focused on your career. There's a chance for a tour—Europe, Asia, the whole thing. It's big, and you can't afford to lose focus."

Elias hesitated, the idea of leaving weighing heavily on him. "I don't know, Kara. I've been working on something else, something important."

Kara raised an eyebrow, unimpressed. "I get it, but this is your career. The world is waiting for you. You can't let a side project distract you."

"It's not a side project," Elias said, frustration building in his voice. "It's something real, something that matters."

But as the days went on, Kara's words echoed in his mind. The idea of going on tour, of returning to his old life before Lena, felt heavy. He was torn between his growing connection with her and the demands of his career.

Back in her studio, Lena kept painting, but the joy she once felt was fading. She missed Elias. Even though they still spent time together, something had changed. He felt distant, his thoughts often elsewhere, even when they were in the same room.

One evening, as the sun began to set, Lena decided she needed to confront her feelings. They had planned to meet at their usual spot on the beach, but as time passed, she felt her anxiety grow.

"Where is he?" she wondered, scanning the shore for any sign of him. She pulled out her phone, hesitating before sending a text: "Are you still coming?"

After a few long minutes, her phone buzzed with a reply: "I'm sorry. Got stuck in the studio. Can we reschedule?"

The disappointment hit her hard. Lena closed her eyes, trying to calm her frustration. "This is happening too often," she thought, her fingers hovering over the phone. She wanted to tell him how much it hurt, how much she missed the way things had been, but the words wouldn't come.

"Sure," she finally replied, her heart sinking as she put her phone away.

The next day, Lena walked around the city, hoping the fresh air would clear her mind. She passed by a small art gallery and noticed a flyer in the window: "Local Artists Showcase: Submit Your Work."

A spark of inspiration lit up inside her. "Maybe this is what I need," she thought, stepping into the gallery.

The owner, an older woman with silver hair and kind eyes, greeted her warmly. "Are you an artist?" she asked, noticing the paint smudges on Lena's hands.

"I am," Lena replied, feeling a new sense of purpose. "I'd love to submit something for the showcase."

Over the next few days, Lena threw herself into her work, determined to create something that showed how she was feeling. The tension with Elias, the uncertainty of their relationship—it all came out in her painting with swirling shades of blue and gray. It was a release, a way to express the emotions she had been holding inside.

But even as she painted, she couldn't stop thinking about Elias. She wondered what he was doing, if he was thinking about her, or if the distance between them was becoming too much to overcome.

Meanwhile, Elias was struggling with his own feelings. He had never felt so conflicted—torn between his music and his relationship with Lena. The chance to go on tour hung over him, reminding him of the life he had before Lena, a life filled with concerts, fans, and endless travel.

One evening, after spending hours in the studio, Elias finally went to Lena's apartment, guitar in hand. He hadn't seen her in days, and the tension between them felt heavy.

When Lena opened the door, she looked surprised but relieved. "Elias!" she said, stepping aside to let him in. "I wasn't sure if I'd see you tonight."

"I'm sorry," he said, setting his guitar down and running a hand through his hair. "Things have been crazy lately. I've been stuck in the studio, and… there's something I need to talk to you about."

Lena's heart raced. "Is this it?" she thought, bracing herself.

"I got offered a tour," Elias said, his voice unsure. "It's a big one. Europe, Asia… I'd be gone for months."

The words hit Lena hard. She had known something was wrong, but she hadn't expected this. "Months?" she whispered, barely able to speak.

Elias nodded. "I haven't decided yet. I wanted to talk to you first."

Lena swallowed, trying to take it all in. "This is your dream, Elias. You've worked so hard for this. I… I don't want to hold you back."

"You're not holding me back," he said quickly, stepping closer. "But I don't want to lose what we have either. I just don't know how to balance it all."

The room fell silent as they both tried to figure out what the future held. Lena's mind raced as she imagined life without him—weeks, maybe even months apart.

"Maybe the distance will make us stronger," she finally said, her voice shaking. "Maybe we need to see if this can survive."

Elias looked at her, torn. "I don't want to lose you, Lena."

"You won't," she whispered, though doubt filled her heart. "We'll figure it out."

But as she spoke, they both knew the road ahead was uncertain, full of challenges neither of them had expected.

That night, they sat together, holding each other close as if their physical closeness could make up for the emotional distance growing between them. But even as they stayed by each other's side, Lena couldn't shake the feeling that they were standing on the edge of something unknown, something neither of them knew how to face.

The Silence Between Them

The days after Elias mentioned the tour were a blur for Lena. She kept herself busy—waking up, working in her studio, and meeting the gallery owner about the showcase—but her thoughts were fixed on the upcoming goodbye.

Elias still hadn't decided, but Lena could feel the tour hanging over them like a storm cloud, darkening every moment they spent together. The easy laughter and creativity they once shared felt strained, as if they were both waiting for the inevitable.

One evening, Lena went back to the beach, sitting on the same weathered bench where she and Elias had first met. The waves crashed against the shore, but the peaceful sound now felt far away, hollow.

Her phone buzzed in her pocket. It was a message from Elias: "Can we talk tonight?"

Lena's heart sank. She knew what was coming. "Of course," she replied, though her fingers trembled as she typed.

A couple of hours later, Elias arrived at her apartment. He looked tired, the spark in his eyes dimmed by the weight of his decision.

"Hey," he said quietly as he stepped inside and shut the door.

Lena gave him a small smile, though it didn't reach her eyes. "Hey."

For a moment, they stood there in silence, thick with unspoken words. Lena gestured to the couch. "Sit?" she offered, but even the casualness of it felt forced.

Elias nodded and sat down, his hands clasped tightly in his lap. Lena sat beside him but left space between them. The gap between them felt vast, reflecting how far apart they had grown emotionally.

After a long pause, Elias spoke. "I've made a decision about the tour."

Lena's heart raced. She had expected this, but hearing it made it real in a way she wasn't ready for.

"I'm going to take it," Elias said, his voice steady but filled with regret. "It's a huge opportunity, Lena. One I can't pass up."

Lena nodded, her heart pounding. "I understand," she whispered, even though she didn't. How could she? How could she be okay with him leaving for months, maybe longer, without knowing what would happen between them?

"I don't want this to be the end for us," Elias said, his eyes pleading. "I want to believe we can make it work, even with the distance."

But Lena wasn't sure. The uncertainty of it all was overwhelming. She looked down at her hands, trying to stay calm. "What if it's too hard?" she asked, her voice trembling. "What if the distance pulls us apart?"

Elias reached out and took her hand. His touch was warm and familiar, but it didn't comfort her like it used to. "I don't want that to happen," he said softly. "But I can't give up this opportunity. You know how much music means to me."

Lena's throat tightened. "I know," she whispered. "And I don't want to hold you back." But even as she said it, she felt the fear creeping in—the fear that no matter how hard they tried, the distance would tear them apart.

Elias held her hand tighter, as if he could feel her slipping away. "We can try, Lena. We can make it work."

She closed her eyes, her heart aching. "But what if we can't? What if we're just setting ourselves up for more heartbreak?"

Silence filled the room, heavy with questions neither of them could answer.

Finally, Lena pulled her hand away, her voice barely above a whisper. "I don't know if I can do this, Elias. I don't know if I can wait for someone who might not come back the same."

Elias's face fell, sadness filling his eyes. "Lena, please… I love you. I don't want to lose you."

Tears welled up in Lena's eyes, but she blinked them back. "I love you too," she whispered, her voice breaking. "But sometimes, love isn't enough."

The words hung between them, final and unchangeable.

Elias sat back, torn between sorrow and understanding. He knew she was right, even though it hurt to admit it. "I don't want this to be the end," he said softly. "But if it is, I want you to know that you've changed me, Lena. You've made me see the world differently. I'll never forget that."

Lena's chest tightened with emotion. "I'll never forget you either, Elias," she said, her voice thick with unshed tears. "You've been my muse, my partner, my everything. But I think… I think we have to let go."

The words broke something inside both of them. They sat in silence for what felt like forever, the weight of their decision settling in the room.

Finally, Elias stood up, his movements slow and reluctant. "I guess this is goodbye," he said softly.

Lena stood too, her heart breaking with every step he took toward the door. "Goodbye, Elias," she whispered, barely audible.

He paused for a moment, as if he wanted to say something more, but instead, he just nodded and walked out the door.

As it closed behind him, Lena felt the full weight of their goodbye crush her. She stood there, staring at the door as tears streamed down her face.

For the first time in a long while, she felt utterly, completely alone.

The Revelation

The days after Elias left stretched into weeks, each one feeling longer and lonelier than the last. Lena found the emptiness in her apartment unbearable. Everywhere she looked, she saw reminders of him—his guitar leaning against the wall, the empty coffee cup he'd always leave by the sink, and the faint echo of his laughter that still lingered in the air.

She threw herself into her art, using her confusion and heartbreak to fill her canvases. The upcoming gallery showcase was the only thing keeping her grounded, but even that felt hollow without Elias there to share it.

Her latest painting sat unfinished on the easel. It was a stormy landscape—dark skies swirling in shades of purple and gray, with waves crashing onto a lonely shore. In the distance, a figure stood alone, almost lost in the chaos. The painting reflected how Lena felt: adrift in a world that once seemed certain but now felt foreign and empty.

Elias hadn't contacted her since that last night. Part of her had hoped he would call or at least send a message, but there had been nothing. The silence was overwhelming, amplifying the emptiness he had left behind.

At night, Lena lay in bed, staring at the ceiling, wondering where he was, what he was doing. She pictured him in some foreign city, surrounded by fans, playing his music in sold-out venues while she sat alone, listening to the quiet hum of the city outside her window. The thought was both comforting and painful—she wanted him to succeed, but it hurt to think of him thriving in a world where she no longer belonged.

Halfway around the world, Elias stood on the balcony of his hotel room, looking out at the unfamiliar city below. The lights sparkled, and the sounds of the nightlife buzzed in the distance, but it all felt far away.

The tour was everything he had ever dreamed of—sold-out shows, screaming fans, interviews with the press. His career was soaring. But even with all the success, something was missing. Every song he played, every melody from his guitar, felt incomplete.

He often thought of Lena, especially late at night. He couldn't shake the image of her standing in the doorway that last night, sadness filling her eyes. He had wanted to stay, but the pull of the tour had been too strong. Now, he wondered if he had made the right choice.

"What have I done?" he muttered, leaning against the railing. Leaving had been hard, but the silence that followed was even harder. He hadn't reached out to her, partly because he didn't know what to say and partly because he was afraid she had moved on.

His phone buzzed with a message from his manager, reminding him of tomorrow's schedule—a day packed with interviews and another show. Elias sighed, feeling the weight of it all. This was the life he had chosen, but it no longer felt like it belonged to him.

In her studio, Lena stood in front of the stormy landscape painting, brush in hand but unable to move. The painting had become a reflection of the storm inside her, but now she was stuck, unable to finish it.

Art had always been her escape, a way to pour her emotions into something beautiful. But now, even that felt out of reach. Tears blurred her vision as she set down the brush, overwhelmed by the pain.

"Why does it still hurt so much?" she whispered to the empty room. She had thought time would heal the wound Elias had left, but it only seemed to grow.

It wasn't just Elias she missed—it was the future they had imagined together. The dreams they had shared, the plans they had made, all gone, leaving an empty space nothing else could fill.

Unable to focus, Lena stepped outside. The evening air was cool, and the sky was painted in soft pinks and golds as the sun set. She walked to the beach, the same one where she and Elias had shared so many moments.

Standing at the water's edge, the waves lapping at her feet, Lena let the memories flood back. She could almost hear Elias's voice, soft and full of warmth, as he whispered promises under the same stars. But now, the sound of the ocean did little to soothe her aching heart.

For the first time, Lena let herself feel the depth of her grief. She had tried to push it away, to focus on her art, but she missed him—missed him in a way that consumed her, as though a part of her soul had been torn away.

"Elias," she whispered, his name barely audible. But the wind carried it away, leaving her standing alone as the sun disappeared into the horizon.

In his hotel room, Elias sat with his guitar in hand, playing a soft, mournful tune. It was the same guitar he had played on stage earlier, where the crowd had cheered and the lights had shone bright. But now, the music felt hollow.

His fingers moved across the strings, playing a melody he hadn't planned—one of the songs he had written with Lena in mind, back when everything felt full of possibility.

He stopped playing and set the guitar down. The music didn't feel the same anymore. Without Lena, it felt like an empty echo of what it used to be.

Elias picked up his phone, his thumb hovering over Lena's contact. He had thought about calling her so many times, but something always stopped him. What would he say? That he missed her? That he regretted leaving? That none of the success mattered without her?

In the quiet of his hotel room, the silence between them felt unbearable. Without thinking too much, he opened a new message and typed a single word: "Hey."

He stared at the screen, his heart pounding as he hesitated. But after a moment, he hit send and waited, the silence of the room pressing in around him.

Breaking Point

The message from Elias came late in the evening, just as Lena was about to turn off her phone. A simple "Hey" lit up her screen, and for a moment, she froze.

Lena stared at the message, her heart racing. She had imagined this moment many times, rehearsing what she would say, how she would respond. Sometimes, she pictured them making up; other times, she imagined accepting it was truly over. But now, with Elias actually reaching out after weeks of silence, she didn't know what to do.

What did it mean? Was it an apology? A casual check-in? Or something else entirely?

Her thumb hovered over the screen, unsure whether to reply or let the silence linger. She wanted to respond—to ask how he was, to pour out everything she had been holding in—but something stopped her. The pain was still too fresh. She wasn't ready to reopen that door, only to face more hurt.

She set her phone down, heart heavy with the weight of unspoken words.

Elias sat on the edge of his bed, staring at his phone, waiting. He hadn't expected Lena to reply right away—if at all—but the silence felt like a growing void.

He had sent the message on impulse, driven by the loneliness that had consumed him since he left. The tour, the crowds, the music— it all felt hollow without her. After the applause faded each night, it was the quiet of his hotel room that brought her back to his thoughts, again and again.

But now, as minutes turned into hours without a response, doubt crept in. Maybe he shouldn't have reached out. Maybe Lena had moved on. Or worse, maybe she didn't want to hear from him.

He picked up his guitar, trying to find comfort in the music, but even that felt wrong. No matter what he played, something vital was missing.

In her studio, Lena was just as conflicted. Days passed, and though she tried to focus on her work, her thoughts kept returning to the unsent reply. She had written dozens of responses in her mind, but none of them felt right. How could she condense everything she felt—months of love, confusion, and heartbreak—into a single message?

It was easier to say nothing. After all, wasn't that what Elias had done? He had chosen his path, and she had let him go, even though it broke her. But now, his message made everything uncertain again. What did he want?

One night, Lena found herself sitting at her kitchen table with a notebook in front of her. Writing had always helped when words failed, and tonight was no different. She flipped to a clean page and began to write.

Elias,

She paused, unsure what to say. She didn't even know if she would send the letter, but she needed to get the feelings out.

I've thought about you every day since you left. I try not to, but everything reminds me of you. I can't even paint without remembering how you used to sit and watch me work, quietly, as if you were part of the art.

She swallowed hard, memories tugging at her heart.

I know how much your music means to you. I would never want to stand in the way of that, but it doesn't make it hurt any less. When you walked out that door, you took a piece of me with you.

Her hand trembled as she wrote, emotions spilling onto the page.

I've tried to move on, but nothing fills the space you left. And now you're reaching out, and I don't know what to do. What do you want from me, Elias? Are you looking to fix things, or just for closure? I don't know if I'm ready for either.

She stopped, feeling overwhelmed. She folded the letter and tucked it into her notebook, unsure if she would ever give it to him. For now, writing it was enough. The words existed, even if he never saw them.

Far away, Elias found comfort in his own unsent words. Late at night, after another long day, he sat at his laptop and began typing.

Lena,

I've wanted to reach out for weeks, but I didn't know how. Every time I tried, the words didn't come. I'm not sure they'll come now either, but I have to try.

He paused, trying to gather his thoughts. He wanted to explain everything—to tell her how much he missed her, how empty the tour felt without her—but no words seemed enough.

I know I hurt you by leaving. I thought I was doing the right thing by going on tour, but now I'm not so sure. Every night, after the show ends, I think about you. About us. About how things might have been if I had stayed.

He sighed, frustration building. How could he express the regret he felt? The loss that followed him every day?

I'm sorry, Lena. For everything. I don't expect you to forgive me, and I'm not sure I deserve it. But you need to know that leaving wasn't easy. It wasn't something I did lightly.

His chest tightened as he thought of their last night together, the pain in her eyes as she said goodbye. He had convinced himself it was for the best, but now, he wasn't so sure.

I miss you. More than I can say. And I hope, wherever you are, you've found peace, even if it's without me.

With a heavy sigh, Elias saved the document, his heart weighed down by all the unsaid words. He didn't send the email. He wasn't ready. Maybe he never would be.

The Last Day

Weeks passed since Elias's message, and the silence between him and Lena lingered, heavy and unbroken. Both were stuck in their own worlds—Lena with her art, Elias with his music—but the memories of what they had lost haunted them.

For Lena, the days leading up to her gallery showcase blurred together. She worked hard to finish her latest pieces, but no matter how much she focused, her mind always drifted back to Elias. The unsent letter remained hidden in her notebook, a burden she carried.

Her assistant, Marina, had been a great help, managing the event's logistics and keeping distractions away. But as the showcase neared, Marina noticed Lena's growing unease.

"You've barely touched that painting," Marina commented, eyeing the stormy seascape still unfinished on the easel. "Are you sure you're ready for the show?"

Lena nodded, though she wasn't sure if she believed it herself. "I'll be fine," she said with a forced smile. "I just need to finish this one. Everything else is ready."

But it wasn't just the painting weighing on her—it was the unsent letter to Elias. She couldn't stop wondering if he was thinking about her too, or if his message had been nothing more than a brief moment of nostalgia.

On the other side of the world, Elias's life seemed perfect on the surface. The tour was a massive success. Every city brought new fans and opportunities. But despite the cheers and the lights, Elias felt lost.

He had started writing new songs, filled with raw emotion. The music wasn't for his audience anymore—it was for him. It was for Lena.

One night, after another sold-out show, Elias stood on a rooftop overlooking the city. The noise of the streets below faded as his mind focused on a single thought: was this really the life he wanted?

He had always dreamed of being a successful musician, but the fame and applause felt empty without Lena.

Pulling out his phone, Elias hovered over her contact, his heart racing. This time felt different. He needed to hear her voice. Before he could second-guess himself, he dialed her number.

Lena was cleaning her brushes when her phone rang. Seeing Elias's name on the screen made her heart stop. She froze, unsure of what to do. Why was he calling now?

She took a deep breath, steadying herself before answering. "Hello?" she said softly.

"Lena," Elias's voice came through the line, and a wave of emotion washed over her. "I wasn't sure you'd pick up."

Lena swallowed hard. "I almost didn't," she admitted. "It's been a while, Elias."

A heavy pause followed, the weight of everything unsaid hanging between them.

"I know," Elias finally said. "I've been thinking about you. About us. I miss you, Lena. I miss everything about us."

His words hit Lena hard. She had longed to hear him say that, but now that he was, she didn't know how to respond.

"You left," Lena whispered, her voice thick with emotion. "You left, Elias. You made your choice, and I had to live with that."

"I know," Elias said, regret clear in his voice. "I thought I was doing the right thing, chasing my dream, but now I'm not so sure."

Lena closed her eyes, fighting back tears. "So, what are you saying? That you regret it? That you regret leaving me?"

"I don't know," Elias said, his voice breaking. "All I know is I can't stop thinking about you. About us. I need to know if there's still a chance."

The silence that followed was suffocating. Lena's heart raced, torn between her love for Elias and the fear of being hurt again.

"I don't know if I can do this again," she said, her voice barely a whisper. "I don't know if I can survive losing you again."

Elias's heart sank. He had always known this might happen—that Lena might have moved on. But hearing it was like a knife to the chest.

"Lena, I—"

"No," Lena interrupted, her voice stronger now. "You left, Elias. You made your choice, and I've been picking up the pieces ever since. I don't know if I can let you back in, just to watch you walk away again."

Elias fell silent, crushed by her words. He had thought reaching out would bring clarity, but it only made things more complicated.

"I understand," he said quietly, his voice filled with emotion. "I understand if you can't forgive me. But I needed to hear your voice. I needed to know if there was still something there."

Lena's eyes filled with tears. Part of her wanted to say she still loved him, but the part of her that had been broken when he left was terrified of getting hurt again.

"I don't know, Elias," she whispered, wiping away a tear. "I just... I don't know."

After the call, Lena stood in her studio, her heart aching. She had always thought hearing from Elias would bring her closure, but it only reopened old wounds.

She looked at the stormy painting on the easel, the one she hadn't been able to finish. Suddenly, she knew what it needed.

With new purpose, Lena grabbed her brush and began to paint. The stormy sky softened into shades of blue and gold, the waves calming as a distant figure took shape. It reflected the crossroads she was at—caught between the past and the future, between holding on and letting go.

Far away, Elias sat in his hotel room, staring at his phone. The silence around him felt heavier than ever. He had tried to fix what he broke, but now he realized that some things couldn't be fixed so easily.

The crossroads they both faced were more daunting than they ever imagined. And as they each stood at the edge of their own paths, the question remained: was love enough to bring them back together, or had they drifted too far apart?

The Aftermath

Lena woke up the next morning, the weight of her conversation with Elias still pressing on her chest. Instead of clarity, the call had deepened her confusion and pain. The showcase for her gallery was just days away, but she felt adrift. As she stared at the painting on her easel, now finished after a late-night burst of inspiration, she realized it symbolized her feelings. The storm in the painting had calmed, yet the tension inside her heart remained.

Marina entered the studio, her usual cheerful demeanor muted as she noticed the shadows under Lena's eyes. "Late night?" she asked gently.

Lena nodded, not ready to share her conversation with Elias. "I finished the painting," she said instead, motioning to the artwork.

Marina's eyes lit up as she approached the canvas. "It's beautiful, Lena. Truly breathtaking." She studied it for a moment and then smiled. "This piece is going to steal the show."

Lena forced a smile but felt uncertain. The painting might be finished, but the story behind it was far from over.

Elias sat alone in his hotel room, replaying the conversation with Lena over and over. Her words cut deeper than he expected. Reaching out had been hard, but he hadn't realized how much he had hurt her.

Now, in the silence of his room, he felt the weight of his choices. The tour, fame, and success felt meaningless without Lena. The thought of losing her for good made him feel sick. He couldn't shake the image of her voice cracking when she told him she wasn't sure if she could forgive him.

Elias picked up his guitar, hoping to find solace in music, but the notes felt empty. He had written songs about love and heartbreak before, but this was different. This was real.

For the first time in weeks, Elias didn't care about the tour or the next show. All he cared about was Lena and whether there was still a chance to make things right.

Two days later, Lena stood in the center of the gallery, watching her paintings being arranged along the pristine white walls. The space buzzed with activity, but Lena felt strangely disconnected. She had spent months preparing for this moment, pouring her heart into each piece, but now that the day was here, it felt distant. The gallery filled with her work, but her mind was elsewhere, tangled in her feelings for Elias.

"You okay?" Marina asked, appearing beside her with a clipboard. "You seem a little... distracted."

Lena nodded, scanning the room. "I'm fine," she replied, though her voice lacked conviction. "Just a lot on my mind."

Marina raised an eyebrow, sensing there was more, but decided not to press. "Well, everything looks perfect," she said with a smile. "You should be proud of yourself, Lena. This is going to be an incredible night."

Lena forced a smile, hoping it would convince Marina—and herself—that she was okay. But deep down, she knew something was missing. The excitement she once felt for the showcase was overshadowed by the unresolved tension with Elias.

As the hours passed and the gallery filled with guests, Lena tried to focus on the event. She greeted art critics, collectors, and friends, all praising her work. But with each compliment, Lena felt more disconnected from the world around her.

Backstage, Elias sat as the crowd's roar grew louder with the opening act finishing. His manager buzzed with excitement, going over the night's performance details, but Elias barely heard him. His mind was miles away, back in the studio with Lena.

He had made up his mind: after tonight's show, he would fly back to her. He couldn't keep running from his feelings or pretending his career was more important than the love they shared. It was time to face the truth: without Lena, nothing mattered.

"Elias, are you ready?" his manager asked, snapping him from his thoughts.

Elias nodded, though he felt unprepared. "Yeah, I'm ready." But in his heart, he knew the only thing he was truly ready for was Lena.

The gallery was packed by the time Lena's showcase peaked. Guests moved from one painting to another, admiring her work and discussing the emotions her art evoked. But as she stood in the center, watching the crowd, a growing emptiness filled her.

She had worked so hard for this moment, dreaming of her art being celebrated. But now, surrounded by admirers, she realized the one person she wanted to share it with wasn't there.

The thought of Elias hit her like a wave, and the room felt suffocating. Lena excused herself from a conversation and slipped outside, needing fresh air.

The cool evening air was a welcome relief as she leaned against the gallery's brick wall, her heart racing. She closed her eyes, trying to breathe steadily, but all she could think about was Elias—how he had said he missed her, the emotion in his voice.

A tear slipped down her cheek, and Lena quickly wiped it away. She had tried so hard to be strong and move on, but now it felt impossible. The truth was, she wasn't over Elias. She didn't know if she ever would be.

Just as she was about to head back inside, her phone buzzed in her pocket. Hesitating, she pulled it out. Her heart skipped a beat when she saw the message.

"I'm coming back to you, Lena. I can't live like this anymore."

Lena's breath caught in her throat as she read the words. She stared at the screen, her mind racing. Was he serious? Was he really coming back?

A flood of emotions washed over her—hope, fear, love, doubt—swirling together in a dizzying storm. She didn't know what to think or how to feel. All she knew was that everything was about to change.

Elias stepped onto the stage, the bright lights blinding him for a moment as the crowd erupted in cheers. But as the music began, all he could think about was Lena. His fingers moved automatically across his guitar strings, but his heart wasn't in it.

He glanced at the clock on the far wall. In just a few hours, he would be on a plane, heading back to her. He had no idea what he would say when he saw her or if she would even want to see him. But he had to try.

Because if he didn't, he would spend the rest of his life wondering what could have been.

Whispers of Yesterday

The air inside the gallery buzzed with excitement, but for Lena, the energy felt distant, like a background hum she couldn't escape. Guests moved through the space, discussing her work, yet all she could focus on was the message from Elias on her phone.

"I'm coming back to you, Lena. I can't live like this anymore."

Her heart pounded as her fingers hovered over the screen, unsure how to respond. Elias had made his decision, but her feelings were a tangled mess. Part of her longed to believe him, to let him back in, while another part—the one that had been broken when he left—urged her to be cautious.

Marina appeared at her side, breaking her thoughts. "Lena, there's someone I want you to meet. One of the most prominent critics in the art world. This could be huge for you!"

Lena forced a smile, nodding, but her mind wasn't on the critic or the gallery. "Give me a moment, okay? I just need to step outside for some air."

Marina frowned, sensing something was off, but she didn't press. "Okay, but don't take too long. This is your night, Lena!"

Lena gave a half-hearted nod before slipping out of the gallery. The night air was cool, and she took a moment to breathe deeply, trying to calm the storm inside her.

She thought of Elias, the night he left, and all the unanswered questions between them. It had taken so long to rebuild herself after he was gone, and just as she felt whole again, he was coming back. But was it too late?

Elias sat in the back of a car, speeding toward the airport. His show had just ended, but he barely remembered it. His mind was only on Lena, the life he had walked away from, and the future he might still have with her.

His phone buzzed with messages—congratulations from fans, updates from his manager about the tour—but he ignored them all. None of it mattered right now. He had made his decision: Lena was the only thing that mattered.

As the car pulled up to the airport terminal, nerves and hope churned in his stomach. He knew he was taking a risk by showing up out of the blue, but he had to see her. He needed to look her in the eyes and tell her how much he still loved her.

After rushing through security, Elias boarded the plane and settled into his seat. He glanced out the window as the city lights began to fade, memories of Lena swirling in his mind. Every moment they had shared—every laugh, every kiss, every fight—played out like a movie.

He had no idea what he would say when he saw her or if she would even want to see him. But he knew one thing for certain: he couldn't go on living without at least trying to make things right.

Back at the gallery, the night was winding down. Guests were trickling out, their chatter fading as the event came to a close. Lena had spent the last hour trying to focus on her art and the excitement surrounding her, but her mind kept drifting back to Elias.

She hadn't replied to his message and wasn't sure if she should. Her heart was at war with itself, torn between the love she still felt for him and the fear of getting hurt again.

Marina approached her again, a bright smile on her face. "Lena, this night has been a huge success. You've made an impression on everyone. I'm so proud of you!"

Lena managed a small smile. "Thanks, Marina. I couldn't have done it without you."

Marina's smile faded slightly as she studied Lena's face. "But something's bothering you, isn't it? You've been off all night. Is it Elias?"

Lena nodded, not bothering to deny it. "He sent me a message," she confessed. "He says he's coming back. I don't know what to do."

Marina's eyes widened. "Wait, coming back? As in, right now?"

"I think so," Lena said quietly, her voice uncertain. "But I don't know if I can trust him. What if he leaves again? What if this is just another impulsive decision?"

Marina placed a reassuring hand on Lena's arm. "You've been through a lot. It's okay to be scared. But if he's really coming back, maybe it's worth hearing him out. Maybe this time, things will be different."

Lena sighed, her mind racing. "Maybe. But I don't know if I can go through all that pain again. What if he's just here to apologize and leaves again?"

The plane touched down, and Elias felt a jolt of adrenaline. He was finally back in the city that held so many memories, both beautiful and painful. It was where he had found love and where he had walked away from it.

As he made his way through the airport, his heart raced. He didn't know if Lena would want to see him, but he had to try. He had to show her he was serious about coming back and fixing what he had broken.

With his guitar slung over his shoulder, Elias stepped out of the terminal and hailed a cab. His hands shook as he told the driver Lena's address, the words feeling both familiar and foreign after all this time.

The ride felt like an eternity, but soon enough, they arrived outside her building. Elias stared up at the windows, wondering if she was inside. The lights were still on, and his heart pounded in his chest as he stepped out of the cab, his legs feeling weak beneath him.

He stood outside for a moment, gathering his thoughts and rehearsing what he would say. But no matter how many times he ran the words over in his mind, they didn't feel right. This wasn't something he could script; he had to speak from the heart.

Elias took a deep breath and walked up to the door.

Inside her apartment, Lena paced back and forth, phone in hand. She still hadn't replied to Elias's message. Her mind spun, emotions in chaos.

Should she call him? Tell him not to come? Or should she let him in and listen to what he had to say?

A knock on the door interrupted her thoughts. Lena froze, her heart leaping into her throat. She knew, even before she opened the door, who it would be.

Slowly, she walked over, her hand trembling as she reached for the knob. Taking a deep breath, she opened the door.

There he was.

Elias stood before her, looking both familiar and different. His eyes, filled with hope and uncertainty, met hers, and for a moment, neither spoke. The silence was heavy, charged with emotions they had both been holding back.

Finally, Elias broke the silence. "Hi, Lena."

Lena swallowed hard, her voice barely above a whisper. "Hi, Elias."

They stood there, on the threshold of something new and fragile. The next words would either pull them together or push them apart forever.

Unfinished Conversations

Lena sat across from Elias in the quiet corner of her apartment. The space between them felt heavy, weighed down by years of unspoken words. Outside, the city pulsed with life, but inside, time seemed to stand still.

"You left without saying goodbye," Lena finally said, her voice steady, though her heart felt anything but. She stared at the floor, avoiding his gaze for now.

Elias shifted in his seat, his hands clasped together, knuckles white from the pressure. "I know," he whispered, his voice hoarse. "I didn't know how to explain it then, and I still don't fully know how to now."

Lena looked up, her eyes sharp. "Try."

Elias took a deep breath, his chest rising and falling with the weight of his words. "I was lost, Lena. The fame, the constant attention—it consumed me. I thought I could handle it, that I could keep you and the life I had while chasing this dream. But I couldn't. I felt like I was suffocating."

"So you chose to leave me behind," Lena said, her voice cracking slightly. She had imagined this conversation a thousand times, but facing it was harder than she had expected.

"I didn't choose to leave you behind," Elias replied quickly. "I was trying to find myself. I didn't know how to be Elias, the musician, and Elias, the man who loved you. I thought you'd be better off without me."

Lena let out a bitter laugh. "Better off without you? Do you know what you did to me when you left? How long it took to put my life back together?"

The pain in her voice hit Elias like a punch to the gut. "I know I hurt you. And I know I can't fix it with an apology. But I'm here now, Lena. I came back because I couldn't stand being away from you anymore."

"But what does that even mean, Elias? You're still living that life. You're still on the road, still caught up in your career. What's changed?"

Elias sighed, running a hand through his hair. "I don't have all the answers, Lena. I just know I want to try. I want to figure it out—with you. If you'll let me."

For a long moment, Lena said nothing. Old wounds felt like they were reopening, but she also felt the pull of love—the love that hadn't quite died, even after all this time. But was love enough?

"I don't know if I can do this again," she said softly, her voice barely audible.

Elias leaned forward, eyes pleading. "I don't expect you to trust me right away. But I'll do whatever it takes to prove that I'm serious, that I've changed."

Lena's heart raced as she looked into his eyes. There was sincerity there, deep regret she hadn't seen before. But there was also fear—fear this could be another fleeting promise, another moment of hope that would leave her shattered.

"We'll see," she said finally, uncertainty filling her voice. "We'll see where this goes. But I'm not making any promises, Elias. Not this time."

The Weight of Time

The days after their conversation were strange, a delicate dance between past and present, between pain and possibility. Lena kept busy with her upcoming gallery opening, burying her doubts and confusion beneath layers of paint and canvas. Yet, no matter how much she tried to focus on her work, Elias's presence loomed large in her mind.

Elias had slipped back into her life quietly but consistently. He didn't push her or ask for more than she could give. He showed up when invited and stayed at a distance when she needed space. It was a balance he seemed determined to maintain, though Lena could feel the weight of his desire for something more—something certain.

One afternoon, Lena found herself at Marina's apartment, sipping tea in the sunlit kitchen. It had become their ritual after the gallery exhibit announcement—a moment to relax before the chaos of opening night.

"So," Marina said, breaking the comfortable silence, her eyes narrowing with curiosity. "How's it going with Elias?"

Lena sighed, pushing her teacup away slightly. "It's complicated. I don't know what to feel half the time. He's trying, really trying. But I don't know if it's enough."

Marina tilted her head thoughtfully. "Do you want it to be enough?"

The question lingered, heavy with meaning. Did Lena want this to work? She had been so focused on the hurt, on protecting herself, that she hadn't asked herself what she truly wanted out of this new chapter with Elias.

"I think I do," Lena said slowly, surprising herself. "But I'm scared. What if he breaks my heart again? What if I can't trust him, or worse, what if I don't even want to anymore?"

Marina leaned forward, her expression serious. "It's normal to be scared, Lena. You're not the same person you were back then. Neither is he. But you have to decide if you're willing to take that risk again."

Lena stared at her tea, swirling the liquid around the cup absentmindedly. "I've worked hard to build my life without him. I'm finally in a good place. And now, he's back, and it feels like everything is shifting again."

"But maybe that's not a bad thing," Marina offered. "You've changed, yes. But maybe what you've built can include him now. Maybe you're stronger together than apart."

Lena considered this. It was true she had rebuilt herself after Elias left. She had become a successful artist, someone independent and sure of her place in the world. But there was still a void, a part of her that longed for the connection she once had with Elias. Could it be different this time? Could they really make it work?

That evening, Elias texted her, asking if she wanted to grab dinner. Lena hesitated, her fingers hovering over her phone screen. Part of her wanted to say no, to keep her distance and protect her heart. But another part—an undeniably curious part—wanted to see him, to see if they could find a way forward.

"Sure," she replied, quickly typing the message before she could change her mind.

They met at a cozy restaurant on the outskirts of the city, one of Lena's favorites. As soon as she stepped inside, her nerves began to settle. Elias was already there, waiting at a small table near the back. He stood when he saw her, smiling that familiar, lopsided grin that still made her heart skip a beat.

"Hey," he said softly, pulling out her chair for her.

"Hey," she echoed, sitting down as he returned to his seat.

For a few moments, they engaged in small talk—nothing too deep or emotional. They spoke about the gallery opening, Elias's latest music projects, and what their friends were up to. But as the night wore on, the weight of unspoken things settled between them.

"I want to ask you something," Elias said, his voice serious. "Why did you agree to meet me tonight?"

Lena blinked, surprised by the question. "I guess I was curious. I wanted to see if this… if we… could be different this time."

Elias nodded slowly, his gaze thoughtful. "And what do you think?"

Lena sighed, leaning back in her chair. "I don't know. I'm still figuring it out." She paused, then added, "I guess I'm just not sure if we can really move past everything that happened."

Elias looked down at his hands, clearly affected by her words. "I get it. I've been thinking a lot about that, too. About how we can rebuild trust and make things right."

Lena studied him for a moment, seeing vulnerability in his eyes. He wasn't the same Elias who had left her all those years ago. He had grown, just as she had. But could growth make up for the damage that had been done?

"Do you think we can?" she asked softly, her voice barely a whisper.

Elias looked up, meeting her gaze with quiet intensity. "I think we can, if we're both willing to try. But it's going to take time, and it's going to be hard."

Lena nodded, her heart heavy with the weight of it all. She knew he was right. There was no easy fix for what had broken between them. But maybe, just maybe, there was still something worth salvaging.

Later that night, back at her apartment, Lena sat on her bed, staring out the window at the city lights below. The conversation with Elias had stirred something deep within her, something she wasn't ready to confront just yet.

But the truth was undeniable: time had changed them both. And now, it was up to her to decide if she was willing to let him back into her life—and into her heart.

Fading Light

The days that followed were filled with unspoken tension, a fragile balance between hope and fear. Lena and Elias continued to see each other, but there was always an undercurrent of hesitation. Something between them had changed—they were no longer the starry-eyed lovers who once believed they could conquer the world together. Time had left its mark on them both.

One evening, as the sun set and the city was bathed in the warm glow of twilight, Lena found herself sitting alone in her studio. The large window overlooked the skyline, and the fading light cast long shadows across the room, mirroring the uncertainties she felt within. She picked up her paintbrush but couldn't bring herself to start. Her thoughts were elsewhere—on Elias, on their tangled past, and on the unknown future that stretched before them.

Her phone buzzed, breaking the silence. It was a message from Elias: "Can I see you tonight?"

She hesitated, unsure if she was ready for another emotional conversation. But something in her heart tugged her toward him. She texted back a simple "Okay."

They met at their old spot by the pier, the place where they had shared so many intimate moments. The water glistened under the moonlight, and the sound of the waves crashing gently against the shore was soothing in its familiarity. Elias was already there when she arrived, leaning against the railing, lost in thought.

"Hey," Lena said quietly as she approached.

Elias turned, offering her a small smile. "Hey."

For a moment, neither of them spoke. They stood side by side, staring out at the water, lost in their own thoughts. Finally, Elias broke the silence.

"Do you ever think about what we could have been?" he asked softly, his voice barely audible over the waves.

Lena felt her chest tighten at the question. She had spent years trying not to think about it, trying to move on from the future they had once imagined together. But now, standing there with him, she couldn't help but let the memories flood back.

"I used to," she admitted, her voice tinged with sadness. "But it hurt too much, so I stopped."

Elias nodded, his expression somber. "I think about it all the time. About what I gave up, what we lost. And I hate that I can't go back and change things."

Lena looked over at him, her heart aching at the raw emotion in his voice. She had spent so long resenting him for leaving and breaking her heart, but now she saw the pain he had been carrying all this time. It didn't make what he had done any less hurtful, but it helped her see him in a different light.

"We can't change the past," she said softly, her eyes fixed on the horizon. "But maybe we can figure out what comes next."

Elias turned to her, his gaze intense. "I want to, Lena. I want to figure it out—with you. But I'm scared too. What if we can't make it work? What if we're just setting ourselves up for more pain?"

Lena let out a soft sigh, the weight of his words settling over her. "I don't know," she said honestly. "I wish I had the answers. But if we're both willing to try, it's worth seeing where this goes."

They stood in silence for a while, the cool breeze ruffling their hair and the sound of the water calming their troubled thoughts. Lena felt a sense of peace wash over her, though it was tinged with uncertainty. She wasn't sure what the future held, but for the first time in a long time, she felt like maybe—just maybe—they could find their way back to each other.

The following week, Elias surprised her by showing up at her gallery. It was early in the morning, before anyone else had arrived, and Lena was in the middle of setting up her new collection. The sight of him standing there, looking so out of place in the sterile, white-walled gallery, made her heart skip a beat.

"I wanted to see your new work," he said with a smile. "Before everyone else gets to."

Lena felt warmth spread through her chest at the gesture. She had always loved how supportive Elias was of her art, even during the toughest times in their relationship. But now, as they stood in the quiet gallery together, something felt different—like they were starting over, with the weight of their shared history still hanging between them.

She led him through the space, explaining the inspiration behind each piece. Elias listened intently, his eyes never leaving her face. For a moment, it felt like old times, like they had slipped back into the easy rhythm of their connection. But there was still a distance between them, a lingering tension that neither knew how to address.

As they reached the final piece in the collection, Elias stopped in front of it, staring at the painting for a long moment. It was one of Lena's most personal works—a large canvas filled with swirling colors and abstract shapes, representing the turmoil she had felt in the years after their breakup.

"This one's about us, isn't it?" Elias asked quietly, his voice thick with emotion.

Lena nodded, her throat tightening as she looked at the painting. "It's about what I went through after you left. All the pain, confusion, and anger... it's all in there."

Elias turned to her, his eyes filled with regret. "I'm so sorry, Lena," he whispered. "I never meant to hurt you like that."

Lena swallowed hard, fighting back tears. "I know," she said. "But it still hurt."

Elias reached out, gently taking her hand in his. "I want to make it right," he said, his voice pleading. "I know I can't erase the past, but I want to be part of your future. If you'll let me."

Lena looked down at their intertwined hands, her heart pounding. She wanted to believe him, wanted to believe that they could make things work. But she wasn't sure if love was enough to overcome everything they had been through.

"I don't know if we can ever go back to the way things were," she said softly. "But maybe we can build something new."

Elias smiled, his grip on her hand tightening slightly. "I'd like that," he said. "I'd like that a lot."

As they left the gallery together, walking side by side through the quiet streets, Lena felt a sense of hope stirring within her. Their love had faded over time, but perhaps, just perhaps, it hadn't disappeared entirely.

Maybe, with patience and understanding, they could find a way to reignite the light that had once burned so brightly between them.

Letters Unread

Lena sat on her living room floor, surrounded by a sea of unopened boxes. The gallery opening was only a few days away, and while most of the pieces had been moved, she still had years' worth of personal items to sort through. After deciding to move into a new apartment closer to the gallery, this seemed like the perfect time to clear out the remnants of her past.

In one corner of the room, a small, weathered shoebox caught her attention. It had been tucked away in the back of her closet, forgotten amid the flurry of packing. Lena picked it up, her fingers tracing the faded edges of the cardboard. She knew exactly what was inside without needing to open it—letters. Dozens of them.

They were all from Elias.

After the breakup, Lena had written letters to him, but she had never sent them. Instead, she kept them tucked away in this box, as if the act of writing would somehow ease the pain. What she hadn't expected was that Elias had done the same.

One evening, years ago, after he had left, he returned to her doorstep, leaving her a box of letters—letters he had written but never had the courage to send. At the time, Lena had been too hurt to read them. She shoved them in the back of her closet and tried to forget they existed.

But now, as she sat cross-legged on her living room floor, the box felt heavier than it had ever been. The weight of unspoken words, of unfinished conversations, pressed down on her as she hesitated, wondering if it was finally time to read them.

With a deep breath, Lena opened the lid. Inside were neatly folded pieces of paper, each one worn around the edges, as if they had been held too tightly, too often. She unfolded the first letter, her heart pounding in her chest as she began to read.

"Lena," the letter began, the ink slightly smudged, as if he had written it in a hurry.

"I don't know where to start, so I'll just say this: I'm sorry. I'm sorry for everything. For walking away, for not being the man you needed me to be. I've replayed that night over and over in my head, trying to understand why I did what I did. And the truth is, I don't have a good answer. I was scared. Scared of losing myself, scared of not being enough for you. So I ran. But it was the biggest mistake I've ever made. I've spent every day since wishing I could take it back, but I know I can't. I just hope, someday, you'll be able to forgive me."

Lena felt her breath catch in her throat as she read his words. She hadn't expected them to hit her so hard, but they did. The raw vulnerability, the regret—everything she had wanted to hear from him back then, but never had. She folded the letter and placed it aside, picking up the next one.

"Lena," the second letter read. "I've been trying to keep myself busy, but nothing feels right without you. I miss you. I miss us. I know I have no right to ask for another chance, but I can't stop thinking about what we had, what we lost. You're in every song I write, every melody that comes to mind. I can't escape you, and I don't want to. You were the best part of my life, and I threw it away. God, I'm an idiot."

Tears welled up in Lena's eyes as she continued reading. She had spent years convincing herself that Elias didn't care, that he had left without a second thought. But these letters told a different story—a story of a man who had been just as lost and broken as she had been.

One by one, she read through the letters, each one more heartfelt than the last. They chronicled his journey, his regret, his longing for a second chance. And as Lena read, she began to see a side of Elias she had never fully understood. He hadn't left because he didn't love her; he had left because he didn't know how to stay.

Hours passed, and by the time Lena reached the final letter, her emotions were raw, her heart aching with the weight of it all. She unfolded the last piece of paper, her hands trembling slightly as she read the words scrawled across the page.

"Lena," it began, "I don't know if you'll ever read this. Part of me hopes you do, and part of me hopes you never have to. I know I've hurt you, and I don't expect you to forgive me. But I need you to know that leaving you was the hardest thing I've ever done. You were my light, my reason for waking up every morning, and walking away from that… it shattered me. I thought I was doing what was best for you, for both of us. But now I see that I was wrong. I should have fought for you, for us. I should have stayed. I'm so sorry, Lena. I love you. I've always loved you. And I always will."

The tears finally spilled over, streaming down Lena's cheeks as she clutched the letter to her chest. It was everything she had needed to hear all those years ago, but now it felt like too little, too late. They had both moved on, both changed. But the love they had shared, the love Elias had spoken of in these letters, still lingered in the air around her.

That night, Lena lay in bed, her mind racing. The letters had opened old wounds, but they had also given her something she hadn't realized she needed—closure. For so long, she had carried the weight of their unfinished story, the unanswered questions, the unresolved pain. But now, she understood. Elias had loved her. He had always loved her. And while it didn't erase the hurt, it softened it.

But what did this mean for them now? Could they still build something new, or had too much time passed? Lena didn't know. But for the first time, she felt a sense of peace, a sense that no matter what happened next, she could finally let go of the past.

The next morning, Elias called. His voice was calm but held a note of uncertainty, as if he could sense the shift in her after reading the letters.

"Lena," he began hesitantly. "I wanted to see if you were free tonight. I was hoping we could talk."

Lena paused, her mind racing with everything she had learned, everything she had felt. She took a deep breath, her fingers tightening around the phone.

"Yeah," she said softly. "I think it's time we talked."

Crossroads

The letter from Elias remained untouched on the nightstand, its edges worn from Lena's fingers tracing over it countless times. Weeks had passed since she found it buried among her mail, yet she couldn't bring herself to read the words he had written. The emotional weight of their reconnection was already heavy, and the thought of confronting the past in his words left her frozen in indecision.

Each morning, she would wake, gaze at the envelope, and tell herself today would be the day. But every night, she fell asleep with the letter still sealed, the answers inside waiting, unanswered.

That evening, as Lena sat curled up on the couch, her apartment felt particularly still. The conversations with Elias had grown more serious recently—deeper, as they navigated their shared history and tried to move forward. They had spent hours talking about everything, yet so much remained unsaid, especially the truths hidden in that unopened letter.

A quiet knock at her door startled her from her thoughts. Pulling her blanket tighter around her shoulders, she opened the door to find Elias standing there, his face etched with a mixture of nervousness and concern.

"Hey," he said softly, his eyes searching hers.

Lena managed a small smile. "Hey, come in."

Elias stepped inside, his presence filling the small living room. For a moment, they stood in silence, the tension between them thick but unspoken. Lena's eyes drifted to the letter, still resting on the nightstand in plain view.

"You haven't opened it," Elias noted quietly, his voice gentle but tinged with something deeper—perhaps a quiet sadness or fear of what his words might reveal.

Lena bit her lip, feeling a surge of guilt. "No, I haven't," she admitted, turning away from him. "I'm not sure if I'm ready."

Elias walked toward the nightstand, his fingers brushing the edges of the letter he had poured his heart into so long ago. His hesitation was palpable, and Lena could sense that the contents of the letter were as daunting for him as they were for her.

"I wrote that letter when I was at my lowest," Elias said, his voice barely above a whisper. "I didn't know how to say goodbye. So I wrote instead. I meant every word at the time, but a lot has changed since then."

Lena swallowed the lump forming in her throat. "Why didn't you send it?"

Elias sighed, running a hand through his hair. "Because I was a coward. I thought I could fix everything by leaving, by putting distance between us. But I was wrong. And by the time I realized that, it felt like it was too late."

The silence stretched between them again, filled with the weight of all they had been through, all they had left unsaid. Lena's fingers trembled as she finally reached for the letter, her hand hovering over it for a moment before she picked it up.

"Maybe we should open it together," she suggested, her voice barely audible.

Elias nodded, his gaze steady and filled with a mixture of hope and trepidation. "If you're ready."

They sat down on the couch, side by side, the letter resting between them like a bridge to the past. Lena took a deep breath, her fingers fumbling slightly as she tore open the envelope. She unfolded the letter, the creases in the paper visible from where it had been held and reopened countless times.

As her eyes began to scan the words, Elias's presence next to her felt both comforting and terrifying. The letter was a window into a time when things between them had been shattered, when their love had been tested and ultimately broken.

Dear Lena,

I don't know if you'll ever read this, and maybe that's for the best. But there are things I need to say, things I never had the courage to tell you when we were face to face. Maybe because I was scared of what the truth might do, to both of us.

I'm sorry. I know that word is probably meaningless after everything that's happened, but I don't know how else to begin. I'm sorry for leaving, for running away when I should have stayed and fought for us. I was lost, Lena—more lost than you could ever know. And in my confusion, I made the worst decision of my life.

The truth is, I left because I was scared—scared of how much I loved you, scared of how much I needed you. You made me feel things I wasn't ready to feel, and instead of embracing that, I ran. It was the biggest mistake I've ever made.

I thought that by leaving, I could figure out who I was without you. But all I found was that I am not whole without you. Every day that passes without you in my life feels like a wasted day, and I'm writing this letter to tell you that I miss you. I miss us.

I don't expect you to forgive me, and I don't deserve a second chance. But I needed you to know the truth—that leaving you was never about not loving you enough. It was about not being brave enough to face my own demons.

If I could turn back time, I would. I would do things differently. But all I can offer now are words, and I know they aren't enough. I just hope you find it in your heart to heal, with or without me.

Always, Elias.

As Lena finished reading, tears welled in her eyes. The raw vulnerability of Elias's words hit her like a tidal wave. All the confusion, the anger, the heartache she had carried for so long suddenly had an explanation. The answers she had been searching for were right there, in his heartfelt confession.

She folded the letter carefully, her hands trembling as she placed it back on the table. Turning to Elias, she saw the same vulnerability reflected in his eyes.

"Why didn't you tell me all of this sooner?" Lena whispered, her voice breaking.

Elias leaned forward, his elbows resting on his knees, his hands clasped together. "I was scared," he admitted. "Scared of what you might say, scared that even after all this time, you'd still hate me."

Lena shook her head, wiping the tears from her cheeks. "I never hated you, Elias. I was just... broken. I didn't understand why you left, and I felt like it was something I had done."

"It was never you," Elias said softly, turning to face her. "It was always me. I was the one who couldn't handle it. And I regret it every day."

The room was thick with emotion as they sat in the silence that followed. Lena could feel the weight of the crossroads they were standing at—one path leading to reconciliation, the other to a final goodbye. The letter had answered so many questions, but it also brought up new ones. Could they move past everything that had happened? Could they truly rebuild something out of the ashes of their love?

"I don't know what happens next," Lena said quietly, her voice raw with emotion. "But I think I'm ready to try."

Elias looked at her, his expression one of both relief and cautious optimism. "I'll take whatever chance you're willing to give me, Lena. I won't let you down this time."

They sat in the stillness of the moment, knowing that the road ahead was uncertain, but also understanding that they had finally reached a place where they could begin again. At this crossroads, they had a choice—to leave the past behind or to let it continue to define them. Lena took a deep breath, feeling the weight of her decision lift, if only slightly.

The future was still unwritten, but for the first time in a long time, she felt like she had the power to choose.

What Was Left Behind

The weeks that followed the night of the letter felt like the calm after a storm. Lena and Elias had finally begun to navigate the delicate process of healing, but the deeper they went, the more they realized their past wasn't just behind them—it had shaped everything about who they were now. Every glance, every word between them seemed to carry the weight of everything left unsaid during their years apart.

Elias started coming over more often, the space between them slowly closing, though neither of them dared to say the words they were both thinking: Can we ever really move on? It was as if they were trying to rebuild a home from bricks scattered from a collapse. Some pieces fit easily, others were damaged, and some were simply missing.

One quiet Saturday morning, Lena found herself standing in front of her closet, pulling down a box she hadn't opened in years. It was dusty, its cardboard edges frayed from time, but inside were the remnants of a past life. She had stored it away the day Elias left, hoping that by burying the physical pieces of their relationship, she could bury the emotional ones too. But that hadn't worked.

Sitting on the floor with the box in front of her, Lena hesitated. Did she really want to open it? What good could come from revisiting those memories?

But something inside her felt compelled to do it. Maybe if she faced what had been left behind, she could finally understand what she was holding onto—and what she needed to let go of.

The first thing she pulled out was a small notebook filled with sketches and notes, some written by Elias, others by her. They used to spend lazy Sunday afternoons sketching together—him designing future buildings, her doodling abstract patterns to pass the time. Flipping through the pages, Lena's heart ached with nostalgia. There was so much love there, so much laughter in those lines.

Next, she found an old concert ticket—the night Elias had surprised her with tickets to their favorite band, just days before everything had started to fall apart. The memory of that night came rushing back. They had danced, kissed, and laughed under the stars as if nothing in the world could touch them. But not long after that night, the cracks had started to appear.

At the bottom of the box was something that stopped her in her tracks: a small photograph of them taken on their first trip together. They were in a park, surrounded by autumn leaves, both smiling widely at the camera, arms wrapped around each other. The image was so full of happiness, the promise of a future they had believed in wholeheartedly.

Lena felt a lump rise in her throat. How had everything gone so wrong? How had they gone from that—the couple in the photograph—to the two people struggling to rebuild their connection now?

Later that evening, Lena sat across from Elias at her kitchen table, the photograph lying between them. He picked it up, his brow furrowing as he stared at it.

"I remember this day," he said quietly, his voice thick with emotion. "We were so sure of ourselves, weren't we?"

Lena nodded, her heart heavy. "Yeah, we were. It feels like a lifetime ago."

Elias put the photo down, meeting her gaze. "What do you think happened to us?"

It was the question that had haunted them both for so long, yet it was the first time either had said it out loud. Lena let the silence hang between them for a moment before answering.

"I think we lost sight of each other," she said softly. "We were so focused on everything else—our careers, our fears, our insecurities—that we forgot about what really mattered. We forgot about us."

Elias sighed deeply, running a hand through his hair. "I know I did. I got so caught up in trying to be everything I thought I was supposed to be that I forgot to be the person you needed."

"We both did," Lena admitted, her voice full of regret. "I kept waiting for you to see me, to come back to me, but I didn't realize that I wasn't really reaching out for you either. I built walls around myself because I was scared of losing you, but in doing that, I pushed you away."

The conversation felt like peeling back layers of an old wound, painful but necessary. For the first time, they were speaking not just about what had happened, but about what they had both failed to do. Lena realized that the pieces of their relationship left behind weren't just memories—they were lessons, things they had to confront if they were going to move forward.

"So what now?" Elias asked, his voice quiet but sincere. "What do we do with what's left behind?"

Lena looked at the photograph again, her fingers tracing the edges. "Maybe we don't try to put it all back together," she said slowly. "Maybe we let some of it go. We're not the same people we were back then, and that's okay. We can't go back to who we were. But maybe we can start over as who we are now."

Elias nodded, a small, hopeful smile crossing his lips. "I like that. Starting over sounds pretty good."

As the evening wore on, the weight between them began to lift, even if just a little. Lena realized that confronting what had been left behind wasn't about reliving the past—it was about understanding it and choosing to move forward anyway. The love they had once shared was still there, buried beneath the hurt, the mistakes, and the time apart. But now, they had a chance to build something new, something different, and perhaps even stronger.

They weren't the couple in the photograph anymore, but maybe that wasn't such a bad thing. Maybe, just maybe, what was left behind could help them find their way forward.

Tides of Change

The days after their conversation about the past felt different. There was a new undercurrent between Lena and Elias— something fragile but promising, like the first rays of sunlight after a storm. They had talked about what was left behind, but now they stood on the edge of something new—what lay ahead.

Elias had begun to open up more, sharing parts of himself that Lena had never fully seen before. He spoke about the years he'd spent alone, the nights when he thought about calling her but didn't. He shared his fears of not being enough, of failing at love, and how much he had missed her. Lena, in turn, found herself doing the same, revealing parts of her heart that had been locked away for so long. For the first time in years, she felt like they were truly seeing each other—not the versions they had projected to protect their hearts, but the raw, real people beneath.

One evening, after another long conversation that stretched into the early hours, Elias suggested something Lena hadn't expected.

"Let's go to the beach," he said, his eyes bright with the spontaneity that had once defined their relationship.

Lena raised an eyebrow. "Now? It's the middle of the night."

Elias grinned. "Exactly. No one else will be there. Just us and the ocean. We used to do stuff like that all the time, remember?"

She did remember. Their early days together had been full of impulsive adventures—midnight drives, random getaways, moments when they felt like the world was theirs to conquer. But life had complicated things. Responsibilities, careers, and expectations had all come between them.

Lena hesitated for a moment before nodding. "Okay, let's do it."

The beach was nearly empty when they arrived, the moon casting a silver glow over the waves. The sound of the ocean crashing against the shore was calming, rhythmic, as if the tides were whispering ancient secrets. Elias and Lena walked side by side along the sand, their footsteps trailing behind them.

"I used to come here after we broke up," Elias admitted after a while, his voice quiet but steady. "I'd sit on the rocks and think. About you. About us. About everything I messed up."

Lena looked at him, surprised. "I didn't know that."

He shrugged, his hands in his pockets. "Yeah, well, I guess I wasn't ready to let go, even though I'd convinced myself I had to. I thought if I came here enough, I'd figure out how to move on. But every time, I just ended up thinking about you."

Lena felt a wave of emotion wash over her, as steady as the tides. "I think part of me never really let go either," she said softly. "I tried to. I told myself I had to, that it was the only way I could move forward. But you were always there, in the back of my mind."

They stopped walking and stood at the water's edge, the cool waves lapping at their feet. For a long moment, neither spoke, but the silence between them was comfortable, almost peaceful. The ocean stretched out before them, vast and endless, and for the first time in a long time, the future didn't feel so daunting.

"Do you think we can really do this?" Lena asked, her voice barely audible over the sound of the waves.

Elias turned to her, his gaze steady and serious. "I think we have to try. I know we've both changed, and it won't be easy. But I don't want to keep looking back anymore. I want to move forward— with you."

Lena looked at him, searching his face for any sign of doubt, but all she saw was sincerity. The fear she had carried with her for so long—the fear of being hurt again, of opening herself up only to be left behind—was still there, but it was quieter now, less overpowering.

"I want that too," she said finally. "But we have to take it one step at a time. We can't rush into things like we did before. If we're going to make this work, we need to be patient with each other."

Elias nodded, his expression softening. "Agreed. One step at a time."

As the night wore on, they sat together on the sand, watching the moonlight dance across the water. The conversation flowed easily between them, sometimes falling into comfortable silences that felt like progress in themselves. It wasn't about finding answers or making promises. It was about being present with each other, about rediscovering the connection they had once shared.

For the first time in years, Lena felt a sense of hope. Things weren't perfect between them, and they still had a long way to go. But sitting there with Elias, the ocean stretching out before them, she realized that maybe, just maybe, they could weather whatever came next. The tides of change were upon them, but instead of fearing the unknown, Lena felt ready to embrace it.

In the Quiet

The days after their late-night beach trip were filled with an unfamiliar stillness. Lena and Elias had fallen into a new rhythm—softer, quieter. There were no grand gestures or passionate declarations of love. Instead, there was a gentle understanding that something was slowly growing between them again, like a seed beginning to sprout after a long winter.

For the first time, Lena didn't feel the urge to rush forward. She didn't need to grasp tightly at what they were rebuilding, afraid it would slip away. Instead, she allowed herself to simply be in the moment. There was something liberating about letting their relationship unfold naturally, without the weight of expectations or past mistakes.

One evening, they found themselves sitting on Lena's balcony, watching the sunset over the city. The sky was painted in hues of pink and orange, and the warm summer air wrapped around them. They didn't talk much; instead, they sat side by side, comfortable in the shared silence.

Lena sipped her tea, her thoughts drifting. It was strange how peaceful she felt now compared to the chaotic rush of emotions she had experienced when Elias first returned. The fear of being hurt again still lingered, but it had faded into the background, replaced by something stronger—trust. It was a different kind of trust than before, born from seeing each other's flaws and choosing to stay anyway.

"You know," Elias said quietly, breaking the silence, "I've been thinking a lot about us lately. About everything that's happened."

Lena turned to look at him, sensing the seriousness in his tone. "What about it?"

He set down his glass, his eyes focused on the horizon. "I guess I've just been wondering how we got here. After everything we've been through, I didn't think we'd ever be able to sit here like this again—together, I mean."

Lena smiled softly. "Neither did I." She paused, letting the thought settle. "But I think that's what makes this so special. We've seen the worst, and somehow, we're still here."

Elias nodded, his brow furrowing slightly as if deep in thought. "I keep thinking about what I could've done differently back then. How I could've fought harder, or stayed, or... something. But I know we can't change the past."

Lena reached out and took his hand, her touch grounding him. "You're right. We can't change it. But I don't think we'd be here now if things had gone differently. Maybe we needed to go through all of that to get to this place."

He looked down at their joined hands, then up at her. "Do you think we can really make it this time? I mean, for the long run?"

It was a question Lena had asked herself countless times. Could they rebuild something lasting after everything they'd been through? But as she sat there with Elias, the quiet between them filled not with tension but with peace, she realized something.

"I don't know," she answered honestly, her voice steady. "But I think we have a better chance now than we ever did before. Because now we know what it takes. We know how hard it can be, and we're both willing to put in the effort. And that's all we can do—try."

The quietness between them wasn't just the absence of noise. It was the space they were giving each other—the space to heal, grow, and become the people they needed to be to love each other the way they deserved. The way they hadn't been able to before.

Elias squeezed her hand gently, his thumb brushing over her knuckles. "I like the quiet," he said softly. "It feels… right. Like we don't have to fill the space with words anymore."

Lena smiled. She knew exactly what he meant. The quiet between them was no longer uncomfortable or awkward. It was peaceful, filled with the understanding that they didn't need to rush into anything. They didn't need to fix everything right away. They just needed to be there for each other, one day at a time.

As the sun dipped below the horizon, casting the city in a soft twilight, Lena felt a sense of calm wash over her. This—sitting in the quiet with Elias—was enough. It was more than enough.

For the first time in a long time, she didn't feel the need to hold on too tightly. She didn't worry about what would happen tomorrow or the day after that. She had learned that love wasn't about grand moments or sweeping gestures. It was about the little things—the quiet moments, the shared silences, and the steady presence of someone who had seen the worst parts of you and still wanted to stay.

And in that quiet, Lena found peace. The tides of change had swept through their lives, but now, in the stillness that followed, they had found something even more valuable—each other.

The Silence Between

The silence between Lena and Elias had changed. Before, it was filled with tension and unresolved feelings, hanging over them like a dark cloud. But now, it felt different—calmer, lighter, like a gentle breeze carrying away their fears.

Lena noticed this one morning as they sat across from each other at breakfast. The clink of silverware, the soft hum of the world outside, and the occasional exchanged glance created a quiet harmony. They didn't need to fill every moment with conversation anymore. The silence spoke volumes, a language they were both learning to understand.

Elias broke the quiet, his voice low and thoughtful. "I used to hate the silence between us," he admitted, staring into his coffee cup.

Lena looked up, curious. "Why?"

He shrugged, a small smile forming. "I thought it meant something was wrong. I tried to fill the space with words, thinking if I kept talking, we wouldn't have to face what we didn't want to deal with."

Lena nodded, understanding. "I felt the same way. If we weren't constantly communicating, it meant we were falling apart. But now… it feels different."

Elias met her gaze. "Yeah, it does. It feels… safe."

Lena smiled, warmth spreading in her chest. "It does. We've found a way to be together without needing to say anything. And that's okay."

The silence had become a refuge, a space where they could exist without the pressure of fixing everything at once. They faced hard conversations head-on but learned to be vulnerable without fear of judgment or rejection. They had learned to sit in the quiet, letting their hearts speak when words failed.

Yet, the quiet also held memories, unanswered questions, and the weight of what still lingered. Sometimes, Lena felt the unspoken things hovering just out of reach. It wasn't tension exactly but an awareness that there were still pieces of their story left untold.

One evening, as they lay side by side on the couch, the weight of those unspoken things settled over them. The flicker of the TV cast soft shadows, but neither paid much attention to the screen. Instead, Lena found herself lost in thought, the silence now feeling less peaceful.

"Elias," she said quietly, breaking the stillness.

He turned to her, his eyes patient. "Yeah?"

She hesitated, unsure if she was ready to dive into her swirling thoughts. But something pushed her forward. "Do you ever think about what would've happened if we never broke up?" she asked softly.

Elias didn't respond right away, processing her question. Finally, he let out a small sigh and nodded. "Yeah, I've thought about it a lot. I used to wonder if we could've made it work if we had just held on longer."

Lena nodded, feeling a lump in her throat. "Me too. I thought about all the ways we could've fixed things. But now I'm not so sure. Maybe we needed that time apart to become who we are now."

Elias reached over, taking her hand. "I think you're right. We weren't ready then. We didn't know how to handle what came between us. But now... we're stronger. We're different."

Lena squeezed his hand, feeling grounded. "I guess we'll never know for sure. But you're right. We're different now. Maybe that's enough."

The silence returned, but it felt lighter, like closure. They didn't need to know what might have been; they only needed to focus on what was in front of them—the present, the quiet, and each other.

In the days that followed, the silence between them continued to grow—not uncomfortably, but in a way that felt like progress. They learned to coexist without constantly needing to fill the space with words. There was beauty in the quiet moments, in simply sitting together.

But Lena knew the quiet wouldn't last forever. Eventually, the unspoken things would resurface, and they would need to confront them. For now, she allowed herself to bask in the peace that had settled over them, knowing they had come a long way from where they started.

The Horizon Beckons

Lena stood at the edge of the cliff, the wind tugging at her hair and the vast ocean stretching out before her. The horizon seemed endless, holding every possibility she had ever dreamed of, yet for the first time, she wasn't sure what she was looking for.

Elias stood beside her, steady and warm but silent. He hadn't said much on the drive up, and Lena didn't push him. This spot—their spot—held memories for both of them. It was where they had come in the early days of their relationship, when everything felt new and exciting, and the future seemed full of promise. It had been their escape, a place to dream about the life they wanted to build together.

Now, it felt like both an end and a beginning.

"It feels different, doesn't it?" Lena said softly, her eyes fixed on the horizon.

Elias nodded, his hands in his pockets as he stared out at the sea. "Yeah, it does." His voice was calm, but a weight hung in the air, as if he felt the significance of the moment too.

They stood in silence, letting the wind and waves fill the space between them. The ocean roared below, crashing against the rocks with a power that reminded Lena of how small they were in the grand scheme of things. It had once been comforting to think their problems were just tiny ripples in the vastness of the world.

But now, standing here again after everything that had happened, Lena felt a mix of nostalgia and uncertainty. So much had changed between them. They weren't the same people who had once stood here dreaming about the future. Maybe that wasn't bad. Perhaps it was time to let go of the past and start dreaming new dreams.

"Do you ever think about the future?" Lena asked, breaking the silence.

Elias glanced at her, a small smile on his lips. "All the time. But it looks a lot different now than it used to."

Lena smiled back, her heart swelling with their shared understanding. "Same here. I thought we had it all figured out, like we knew exactly where we were going. But now… I'm not so sure. And I think that's okay."

Elias looked at her for a long moment, his eyes soft and filled with something Lena couldn't quite name. "I think it is. We don't need all the answers right now. We just need to keep moving forward."

The horizon beckoned, vast and open, filled with the unknown. For the first time in a long time, Lena didn't feel afraid of it. The future wasn't something to fear—it was something to embrace. There were still questions and unresolved issues between them, but that was okay. They didn't need to rush to the finish line. They had learned that the journey—the ups and downs, the quiet moments and chaos—held the real beauty.

"What do you want, Elias?" Lena asked, her voice steady but curious. "What do you see when you look ahead?"

Elias turned to her, his gaze unwavering. "I see us," he said simply. "I don't know where we'll end up or how long it'll take, but I see us figuring it out. Together."

Lena felt warmth spread through her chest at his words, her heart settling into a quiet certainty. There was no grand declaration, no sweeping gesture—just a simple truth spoken in the stillness of the moment.

"Me too," she whispered, her voice barely audible over the wind. "I see us too."

They stayed there for a while longer, at the edge of the world they once knew, letting go of the dreams they had outgrown. The horizon called to them, not with promises of perfection, but with the possibility of something real, something worth fighting for.

As they walked back to the car, hand in hand, Lena realized the future didn't scare her anymore. The horizon might be unknown, but it was theirs to explore. And wherever it led them, they would face it together.

The Last Note

The autumn air had turned crisp, and leaves danced down from the trees like confetti, painting the streets in shades of amber and gold. It was the kind of day alive with possibilities, yet Lena wandered through the park, feeling a heaviness in her heart. Despite the beauty around her, unexpressed emotions lingered just beneath the surface.

Elias had left for a weekend trip to visit his family, and though she knew he would be back soon, the distance between them—both physical and emotional—felt greater than ever. In moments like this, alone with her thoughts, the silence between them stretched longer, filled with things they hadn't said.

Lena paused on a bench, looking out at the pond where ducks glided effortlessly across the water. The tranquility of the scene sharply contrasted with her inner turmoil. She pulled out her phone, scrolling through their recent messages, searching for comfort in their exchanges. There were sweet texts, laughter shared over silly memes, and deep conversations late into the night. But there were also echoes of their past—the misunderstandings, the pain, and unresolved issues that still needed attention.

Taking a deep breath, Lena decided it was time to confront the feelings she had been avoiding. She reached into her bag and pulled out her journal, a place where she could freely express her thoughts without judgment. Opening it to a blank page, she began to write:

"Dear Elias,"

The words flowed easily, spilling onto the page as if waiting for her courage to express them. She wrote about the uncertainty that crept in when they were apart, the nagging fear that they were still fragile, still on shaky ground despite how far they had come. She wrote about her love for him, deep and unwavering, but also about her longing for something more—clarity, commitment, and a shared understanding of their future.

As she poured her heart out, Lena felt a weight lifting, her thoughts finally taking shape. She wanted to share this with Elias, to let him know how deeply she cared, but also how much she needed them to be on the same page.

After finishing her letter, Lena folded the page neatly and slipped it into an envelope, sealing it with a sense of finality. She knew she wouldn't send it right away; instead, she wanted to give it to him when he returned—a tangible piece of her heart laid bare for him to hold.

With newfound purpose, she stood up from the bench, taking a moment to soak in the beauty of the day. The sun began to set, casting a warm glow over the park. As she walked, her mind drifted to memories of Elias—the way his laughter filled a room, the softness in his gaze when he looked at her, and the feeling of safety he had cultivated around them.

Lena knew they had come a long way, but she also understood there were still hurdles to overcome. They needed to talk openly about their hopes and fears and the future they wanted to build together. The letter wasn't just a reflection of her heart; it was a call to action.

Later that evening, she prepared dinner for herself, her heart lighter as she moved about the kitchen. The smell of garlic and herbs filled the air, but even the comforting aromas couldn't quite shake her longing for Elias. The quiet of the apartment felt palpable, and she wished for the sound of his laughter to fill the empty spaces.

Just as she was about to sit down to eat, her phone buzzed on the counter. Lena rushed over, her heart skipping a beat as she saw Elias' name on the screen.

"Hey, beautiful. I just got back. Can I come over?"

Her heart leapt at the thought of seeing him, and she quickly replied, "Of course! I'd love that."

A short while later, she opened the door to find Elias standing on her doorstep, a bright smile lighting up his face. The sight of him made her heart swell, the distance of the last few days melting away.

"I missed you," he said, stepping inside and wrapping his arms around her.

"I missed you too," Lena replied, breathing in his familiar scent—woodsy and warm, like home.

As they settled on the couch, Lena felt a flutter of nerves in her stomach. It was now or never; she needed to share the letter with him. She reached for the envelope, her hands trembling slightly as she handed it to him.

"What's this?" Elias asked, curiosity dancing in his eyes.

"Just something I wrote while you were gone. I want you to read it."

Elias took the envelope and opened it carefully, pulling out the folded page. As he began to read, Lena felt her heart race, a mix of anticipation and anxiety swirling within her. She watched his expression change as he absorbed her words, curiosity giving way to deeper understanding.

When he finished reading, he looked up at her, his gaze intense. "Lena, this is... wow."

She bit her lip, unsure how to interpret his reaction. "Is it too much?"

"No, not at all," he replied quickly. "It's just... I had no idea you were feeling this way. I'm glad you wrote it down."

They fell into a conversation that felt both vulnerable and electric. Lena spoke about her fears and hopes for their future, while Elias opened up about his own insecurities and his desire to move forward with her. The air was filled with honesty, and the silence that had once been heavy between them felt lighter, punctuated with laughter and shared understanding.

As they talked late into the night, Lena realized that this was the last note she needed to write. It wasn't the end but rather the beginning of a new chapter in their relationship—one grounded in openness and communication.

Love in the Wind

The morning sun poured through the window, casting a warm glow over the living room. Lena stirred awake, the soft rustle of leaves outside beckoning her to the world beyond. It had been a few weeks since Elias read her letter, and during that time, they had shared countless conversations, each one deepening their connection. The silence that once felt heavy now wrapped around them like a comfortable blanket, filled with trust and understanding.

As she sat up and stretched, Lena smiled at the sight of Elias still asleep on the couch, cozy blankets draped over him from their late-night talks. Her heart warmed at how far they had come—not just as individuals but as partners.

After a quick breakfast, Lena decided to surprise Elias. She tiptoed into the kitchen, her heart fluttering with excitement. She brewed fresh coffee and set out pastries from their favorite bakery. The sweet scent mingled with the aroma of the coffee, and she felt joy at bringing him these small moments of happiness.

Once everything was ready, she went to wake him, gently shaking his shoulder. "Hey, sleepyhead. Time to rise and shine."

Elias stirred, blinking up at her with a sleepy smile. "Is that the smell of coffee? You know me too well."

Lena laughed, handing him a steaming cup. "I had a feeling you might appreciate it."

As they settled at the table, the morning sun illuminated their faces. Lena felt an overwhelming sense of contentment wash over her. They talked and laughed over breakfast, the weight of their past dissipating with each shared word. A lightness filled the air, refreshing and new, as if they were embarking on an exciting adventure together.

After breakfast, they decided to take a walk in the nearby park. The autumn foliage was in full display, vibrant colors transforming the landscape into a canvas of red, orange, and yellow. As they strolled hand in hand, a cool breeze danced around them, carrying the laughter of children playing and the distant sound of a musician strumming his guitar.

"I love this time of year," Lena said, her eyes sparkling as she took in the beauty around them. "Everything feels so alive."

Elias squeezed her hand, a smile playing on his lips. "It really does. And it's nice to enjoy it together."

They wandered deeper into the park, finding a secluded spot beneath a grand old oak tree. The leaves rustled in the breeze, creating a soothing symphony around them. Lena felt an urge to capture this moment, to hold onto the peace they had found together.

"Can I share something with you?" Lena asked, sitting on a bench.

Elias looked at her, his expression curious and attentive. "Of course."

"I've been thinking about how far we've come and the things we've been through. It hasn't always been easy, but I wouldn't trade it for anything," Lena confessed. "You've taught me so much about love, patience, and embracing the unknown."

Elias leaned closer, his eyes softening as he listened. "I feel the same way. You've challenged me to be better, to open up and trust. I can't imagine my life without you."

Their hands intertwined, fingers weaving together to cement their connection. The wind picked up, swirling around them and carrying a sense of renewal and hope. Lena felt a rush of gratitude for their journey, for the moments that had led them here.

"I've been thinking," she said, her voice steady but filled with emotion. "About what the future holds for us. I want us to keep exploring this and build something real together."

Elias smiled, excitement glimmering in his eyes. "I want that too. I want us to face whatever comes our way, side by side."

As they sat beneath the oak tree, the world around them felt suspended in time. The rustling leaves seemed to whisper promises of new beginnings, and the horizon beckoned them forward.

"You know, I think love is a lot like the wind," Lena mused, glancing at Elias. "It can be gentle and calming, but also fierce and unpredictable. It moves in ways we can't always understand, but it's always there, guiding us."

Elias nodded, his gaze fixed on her. "And just like the wind, love can carry us to places we never imagined. It can lift us up, push us forward, and sometimes even surprise us."

In that moment, the connection between them deepened, a silent understanding passing between them. They had weathered storms together, faced uncertainties, and emerged stronger.

As the sun began to set, casting golden hues across the sky, Lena and Elias shared a quiet moment, soaking in the beauty surrounding them.

"Whatever comes next, I'm ready to face it with you," Lena said, her voice barely above a whisper.

Elias turned to her, his expression earnest. "And I with you. No matter what, we'll make it through together."

With that, they shared a gentle kiss, the world around them fading away. In that moment, they were simply Lena and Elias, bound by love and a future awaiting them.

As they walked home, hands entwined, the wind danced around them, carrying the promise of tomorrow. They had found each other in the quiet, learned to embrace silence, and discovered a love that thrived in the spaces in between.

In the distance, the horizon stretched on, an open invitation to whatever lay ahead—a future filled with hope, laughter, and endless possibilities.

Together, they were ready to embrace it all.

Chapter 23: Love in the Wind serves as a beautiful conclusion to Lena and Elias' journey. It captures the essence of their growth, deepened connection, and readiness to face the future together. Acknowledging love's unpredictable nature, this final chapter leaves readers with a sense of hope and the belief that true love can weather any storm.

With their story ending on a high note, the novel closes, leaving a lingering warmth in the heart—a reminder that love, like the wind, is both powerful and freeing.

The End

Summary of Eternal Whispers

"Eternal Whispers" is a poignant exploration of love, vulnerability, and the transformative power of communication through the experiences of Lena and Elias. Their story unfolds against a backdrop of personal struggles, past heartaches, and the undeniable connection that binds them. This journey, filled with emotional highs and lows, captures the essence of navigating a relationship marked by silence, misunderstandings, and ultimately, growth.

The novel opens with Lena standing at the edge of a cliff, contemplating her past and the relationship she shares with Elias. The ocean, vast and seemingly endless, mirrors the complexity of her emotions. This moment signifies the weight of unspoken words and unresolved feelings lingering between them. Despite the beauty surrounding her, Lena feels an unsettling sense of uncertainty about her future. Elias stands beside her, embodying both support and distance, as they reflect on the memories forged in this special place, a refuge from the world that once held promise and excitement.

In their early days, Lena and Elias had shared dreams and aspirations, envisioning a future filled with love and adventure. However, time has altered their connection, introducing doubt and a sense of fragility. As they stand together, Lena realizes that change is inevitable; their past selves no longer align with who they are today. This realization becomes a turning point, prompting them to embrace the possibility of forging new dreams together.

The narrative unfolds with Lena's growing introspection and her decision to confront the feelings she has been avoiding. When Elias leaves for a weekend trip, the distance between them amplifies the silence that has come to define their relationship. Lena's emotions swell as she wanders through the park, capturing the contrast between the vibrant autumn landscape and the heaviness in her heart. In this solitude, she begins to understand the importance of expressing her feelings and reflecting on the unaddressed issues that have lingered in the shadows.

Lena's journey takes a significant turn when she decides to write a letter to Elias, an act of courage that represents her commitment to vulnerability. The letter encapsulates her fears, desires, and hopes for their future together. As she pours her heart into her journal, she acknowledges her love for Elias while also seeking clarity and understanding. This cathartic exercise allows Lena to articulate her emotions and creates a tangible piece of her heart for Elias to hold.

When Elias returns, Lena eagerly shares the letter with him, and the moment marks a pivotal juncture in their relationship. The letter serves as a bridge, connecting their unspoken thoughts and feelings, and propelling them into deeper conversations. As they explore their emotions, they begin to unravel the complexities that have caused them to drift apart. The atmosphere shifts from one of uncertainty to openness, as they confront their past and envision a shared future.

Their interactions become rich with honesty, revealing layers of vulnerability that had previously been buried. Through heartfelt discussions, they express their fears and desires, allowing each other to see their true selves. Lena learns to articulate her longing for commitment, while Elias shares his insecurities about the future. This newfound openness transforms the silence that once weighed heavily on them into a comfortable space of understanding and trust.

The beauty of the autumn season serves as a metaphor for their evolving relationship. As they stroll through the park, surrounded by vibrant colors, Lena reflects on how love can be both nurturing and unpredictable. Their walks become an essential part of their reconnection, filled with laughter and shared moments that reinforce their bond. Each conversation brings them closer, as they explore their individual journeys and how those journeys intertwine.

As the story progresses, the theme of love as a guiding force emerges prominently. Lena and Elias discover that love is not just a feeling but a commitment to navigate life together, regardless of the challenges they may face. They learn that vulnerability and communication are vital components in building a lasting relationship. The letters and conversations serve as tools for growth, allowing them to dismantle the walls they had built around their hearts.

In the latter chapters, the narrative delves deeper into Lena and Elias's hopes for the future. Their discussions become increasingly focused on what they want to build together. Lena expresses her desire for a future filled with shared experiences, while Elias emphasizes the importance of facing challenges as a united front. Their connection solidifies as they acknowledge the strength they derive from one another, realizing that they can tackle life's uncertainties together.

The climax of "Eternal Whispers" occurs during a serene afternoon in the park, where they find solace beneath a majestic oak tree. The moment encapsulates their journey of growth, as they reflect on how far they have come and the challenges they have overcome. Surrounded by the rustling leaves and gentle breeze, they share a deep conversation about their relationship's future. Lena articulates her desire to keep exploring their connection, while Elias echoes the sentiment, expressing his commitment to facing whatever lies ahead side by side.

This chapter resonates with the idea that love is a journey, not a destination. Lena's metaphor of love as the wind encapsulates the unpredictable nature of relationships—sometimes gentle, sometimes fierce, but always present. Elias's agreement solidifies their shared understanding of love as a force that can guide them to unexpected places, pushing them toward growth and new experiences.

As the sun sets on this beautiful day, the couple shares a tender kiss, symbolizing their readiness to embrace the future. The moment feels like a culmination of all their efforts—an acknowledgment of their love and a promise to continue navigating life's journey together. This profound connection they share is both grounding and liberating, allowing them to step into the unknown with confidence.

The closing chapters of "Eternal Whispers" leave readers with a sense of hope and warmth. As Lena and Elias walk hand in hand, the horizon stretches before them, an open invitation to whatever lies ahead. The landscape of their love, filled with both challenges and joys, reflects their commitment to growth and exploration. The culmination of their journey is not just about finding resolution but about embracing the ongoing adventure of love—a love that is resilient, nurturing, and transformative.

In the end, "Eternal Whispers" serves as a poignant reminder that true love can weather any storm. It highlights the beauty of vulnerability, the importance of open communication, and the strength found in shared experiences. Lena and Elias's story resonates with readers, encouraging them to reflect on their own journeys of love and connection. The novel concludes on a hopeful note, leaving a lasting impression of the power of love to transcend obstacles and create lasting bonds.

As Lena and Elias stand on the precipice of their future, they embody the idea that love, much like the wind, is both powerful and freeing. Their journey reflects the essence of human connection, illustrating that the whispers of the heart can guide us through even the most turbulent times. With a blend of warmth, vulnerability, and hope, "Eternal Whispers" invites readers to believe in the enduring nature of love and the endless possibilities it can bring.

The End

More Books by the Author

A prolific author, Divyam has published numerous comprehensive guides aimed at helping individuals and organizations navigate the complex world of digital marketing, branding, and web development. His notable works include:

- Agarwal, Divyam (1 January 2024) "Digital Dynamo: Navigating the Landscape of Digital Marketing" Self-Published (English) ISBN: 978-93-6123-996-0
- Agarwal, Divyam (15 January 2024) "Mastering SEO: A Comprehensive Guide to Dominating Search Engines" Self-Published (English) ISBN: 978-93-6128-989-7
- Agarwal, Divyam (31 January 2024) "Mobile Mastery: A Comprehensive Guide to Dominating the Mobile Marketing Landscape" Self-Published (English) ISBN: 978-93-340-0427-4
- Agarwal, Divyam (1 February 2024) "Social Symphony: A Comprehensive Guide to Mastering Social Media Marketing" Self-Published (English) ISBN: 978-93-6128-219-5
- Agarwal, Divyam (15 February 2024) "Automate to Captivate: A Comprehensive Guide to Marketing Automation" Self-Published (English) ISBN: 978-93-340-0570-7
- Agarwal, Divyam (29 February 2024) "The Art and Science of Advertising: Mastering the Marketing Game" Self-Published (English) ISBN: 978-93-340-0927-9
- Agarwal, Divyam (1 March 2024) "Brand You: Mastering the Art of Personal Branding and Press Releases" Self-Published (English) ISBN: 978-93-6128-418-2
- Agarwal, Divyam (15 March 2024) "Web Mastery: A Comprehensive Guide to Modern Web Development and Design" Self-Published (English) ISBN: 978-93-340-1361-0
- Agarwal, Divyam (1 April 2024) "The Influencer Code: Mastering the Art and Science of Influencer Marketing" Self-Published (English) ISBN: 978-93-6128-565-3
- Agarwal, Divyam (1 June 2024) "Omnichannel Marketing: Bridging the Gap Between Online and Offline Experiences" Self-Published (English) ISBN: 978-93-340-9587-6

www.ingramcontent.com/pod-product-compliance
Lightning Source LLC
La Vergne TN
LVHW011035200726
843509LV00011B/1282